Praise for Beth Williamson's The Prize

4.5 Stars! "Gorgeous cowboys and nasty bad guys make Williamson's second Malloy tale impossible to put down. This sexy, fast-paced Old West story thrills with hair-raising adventure and wry humor." ~ *Susan Mitchell, Romantic Times Book Reviews*

"The Prize by Beth Williamson was an emotionally charged highly sensual read that I took great pleasure in reading. I found myself immersed in the plot from beginning to end. Totally satisfied, I can't wait to read the next installment of Ms. Williamson's wonderful family, the Malloy's." ~ *Talia Ricci, Joyfully Reviewed.com*

4.5 Blue Ribbons "...THE PRIZE is the second book in the Malloy family series and is every bit as good as the first...With a surprise ending that brought tears to my eyes THE PRIZE is a book not to be missed and Beth Williamson is an author to watch out for in the future." ~ *Dina Smith, Romance Junkies*

THE PRIZE

Beth Williamson

A SAMHAIN PUBLISHING, LTD. publication.

Samhain Publishing, Ltd.
2932 Ross Clark Circle, #384
Dothan, AL 36301

This title has been previous published with another publishing house.
First Samhain Publishing, Ltd. electronic publication: May 2006
First Samhain Publishing, Ltd. print publication: August 2006

DEDICATION

To my muse sister and friend, Christy. This one's for us.

CHAPTER ONE

Cheshire, Wyoming, March 1884

Jack Malloy hung his head over the washbasin and tried desperately not to retch. The lingering effects of his nightmare gripped him like eagle talons digging into his head and stomach, and most especially his heart. He could hardly pull in a breath. The weight pushing down on his chest was incessant, staggering. His hands were shaking, he stank like sweat and fear, and he could barely stand up. Jesus, how did he get to be such a wreck?

After the first urge passed, he grabbed the basin and the pitcher of cold water and stumbled back to his bed in the gray light of dawn. The sheets were damp and smelled worse than he did—if that were possible—but he sat anyway. Setting the pitcher on the nightstand, he put the basin on the floor and leaned over to put his head between his knees, hoping to dispel the urge to vomit.

It had become a nightly routine for him. Not just nightly, actually. Every time he tried to sleep, it was the same, whether in the afternoon or the middle of the night. His dreams became nightmares. The nightmares became absolute terror.

Sleep had become a curse in Jack's vocabulary, because no matter what he did, the nightmares would not cease.

He tried to shake them off and go back to sleep. However, it was easier said than done. He had to wait until the shakes passed, until the nausea passed, before he could wash. By that time, his sheets had dried off somewhat so he could crawl back in his hovel to hide. Even then, he didn't sleep. Half the time, he felt a burning deep in the back of his throat from the bile that threatened.

Instead of simply ignoring his nightmares, he tried to avoid them completely. He snorted at the methods he'd tried and failed at. There was the time he tried drinking himself stupid with some whiskey, which only gave him a pounding headache to add to his list of sleep problems.

Jack had tried his mother's medicinal laudanum, which just made his dreams much more vivid and nearly sent him screaming from the house. That was an experience he would never repeat even if half his leg was severed. Just the thought of those heightened nightmares made him shudder.

Next he tried working himself to death for fifteen hours a day for a week. Unfortunately that didn't work either. He was so overtired he hardly slept and still woke up twice to nightmares.

It seemed hopeless, and there was nobody to turn to, because no one in his family knew why he was having nightmares. There was too much shame attached to the "why" to tell his family what was happening. He was a grown man, twenty-four years old; he should be able to deal with bad dreams.

These were more than bad dreams. They were tearing his soul to pieces. There wasn't a part of him that didn't hurt, either physically or emotionally. Jack avoided even thinking too much anymore, it was just too hard. Life was too hard.

With one last hitch over the basin, the urge to bring up yesterday's supper finally passed. He picked up the pitcher and poured some water into it. Dipping a washrag in, then squeezing it out, he began to wipe off the sweat. His normally brown, wavy hair was nearly soaked with it. As the goose bumps ran up and down his spine from the chill in the air, he was embarrassed to feel tears pricking his eyes. He was hanging on to the end of a rope, clawing to keep his sanity, but it was so damn hard. And he was so alone.

Except, of course, in his nightmares. For that particular pleasure, he was joined by Rebecca Connor, his sister Nicky's best friend. Rebecca had survived some brutal treatment herself, and her image, her screams, haunted his dreams although he hadn't been there to witness any of her experiences. Apparently his imagination could conjure up images for him. Lucky him. As if his own nightmares weren't enough.

If he ran into Rebecca again, he didn't know what he'd do. Just seeing her would probably send him into apoplexy. Like a dream monster coming to life. It wasn't fair to her. *She* wasn't truly the cause of his nightmares, he was, but she was there and her experiences mixed with his, forming a strange bond of pain and terror. Only she didn't know about it. It made his situation that much harder. Rebecca and Nicky were as close as sisters. Jack did everything he could to avoid her, but his subconscious had other ideas. Rebecca was his nightmare bride whether he wanted her or not.

He set the washrag in the basin and leaned back on the bed, trying not to shake too much. He rubbed his eyes with the heels of his hands. His eyes felt like they'd been plucked out, dipped in sand and stuck back in his head.

"Jack?"

He nearly fell off the bed in surprise. His sister Nicky, now seven months pregnant, stood at the door peering at him through the gloom. Her wavy reddish brown hair was in a fat braid resting on her shoulders and her normally smooth gait clunky because of her belly.

"Are you okay?"

This was *not* what he needed. Nicky had been eyeing him suspiciously for the past week since she'd been at the Malloy family ranch visiting. He was already lying to his mother, so he'd lie to Nicky too. More shame on his already broken back.

"I'm fine. Go back to bed."

She ignored him and walked in anyway, immediately wrinkling her nose. "Whew. What are you doing in here? It smells like a whorehouse."

Jack was too exhausted to be polite and figured maybe sarcasm might send her back to her room. "You caught me. I've been secretly running a whorehouse from my bedroom."

"Funny, Jack, very funny." She sat on the edge of the bed and made a quick grab for one of his hands.

He was still muzzy from lack of sleep and wasn't fast enough. She sucked in a breath.

"Hell, Jack, your hand feels like a dead fish."

"You keep passing out the compliments and I'm going to get a big head. You need to get out of here. You realize I'm only wearing my drawers, right?"

Get out. Now, Sissie.

He tried to yank his hand back, but she wouldn't let go. He sighed. "You're going to speak your peace anyway, so you might as well get it over with." Damn stubborn, cussed woman.

"I was half-asleep when I heard the most painful sound I've heard in a long time. Reminded me of a time I'd like to forget... It was you, Jack. Dreaming. And I don't think it was a *good* dream. I'm not sure how long you've been like this. I can't help wondering if my return didn't cause whatever it is. I can feel it, in here." She touched a fist to her heart, her green eyes lit with real, honest-to-God worry. "I'm worried about you, Jackaroo."

He shook his head. "No, you didn't do anything. Nothing is wrong, so leave me be."

Liar.

"I can't. You're not sleeping. You have luggage under your eyes that could rival any debutante's. Your hands shake. Your temper is short. You—"

He slashed the air with his hand, cutting her off. He didn't need a list of his problems. "I get the point."

Her hands tightened on his. "Jack, please trust me," she whispered. "Please."

"There's nothing to tell." How could he ever tell her the brutal truth? *No one* knew what had happened to him, and he planned to keep it that way. The revelations last fall when Nicky returned had made his childhood memories resurface with a nasty vengeance. A vengeance that was stealing his sleep. And his life.

"I want to help you."

He snorted. "There's nothing you can do for me, Sissie. Leave it be."

"I can't."

She sounded perilously close to tears. That wasn't going to work either. She cried at the drop of a hat since she'd been pregnant. Besides, there was no way in hell Jack would *ever* tell her about his problems. He just couldn't.

"And I can't talk about it."

She squeezed his hand hard between hers. "I understand. Talking can be harder than anything else you have to do in your life. But I'm here and I'm listening."

He reached out and pulled her into a hug, swallowing a small sob that had somehow made its way up his throat. Jesus

Christ. He cried nearly as much as she did lately. Releasing her quickly, he sat back against the pillows, hoping the minimal lighting hid the naked grief in his wet eyes and the shaking in his body.

"Do you remember when we decided to be gold miners?"

Nicky's soft question knocked him for a loop. The memories of going prospecting with her and Logan were so clear he thought he could reach out and touch them. It was the first time he'd had the urge to smile in a very long time. The memory tasted as sweet as a peppermint stick.

"Sure do."

"The three of us heading out with a shovel, a sack and a lantern. You were the one that convinced us there was gold in the hills behind the house. We had stars in our eyes the whole day. After two hours, we had blisters and were whining to beat the band, but you convinced us to keep going. We brought home some granite, and a piece of sparkly quartz or two, sure we were to be filthy rich. Mama ooohed and aaahed over the rocks like she'd never seen the like."

She paused and rubbed her thumbs on the back of his hand. "And you know what? I was rich that day. We loved you, you were our big brother, and we believed in you. Even if all we had was a sack of rocks. They were gold to us. *You* were gold to us, Jack. I know I'm not supposed to play favorites with my brothers, but you know that you were the sun, the moon and the stars to Logan and me. We would have done anything for you. I'll still do anything for you. I love you, big brother. It's time for you to believe in me. To let me help you."

She took a deep shuddering breath that he echoed, trying to get a hold on his runaway emotions. Goddamn interfering sister. Why couldn't she just leave him be?

"So I'd like you to come back home with me to the Bounty Ranch for a while. With me being unable to help, and since we can't afford any hired hands yet, Tyler is finishing the addition to the house with only Noah's help. He's nearly sick with exhaustion trying to keep up with his regular chores plus the addition, and he's tired of me nagging him, as he puts it. We need help, Jack. Especially someone with your skill with wood. And I want to bring the cradle home that you made for the baby. I can't wait for Tyler to see it. Please say you'll come. I shouldn't be driving the wagon so pregnant anyway."

No wonder Tyler called her magpie. Once you took the cork out, she just kept right on going. The word "no" danced on his tongue, eager to jump out. But he just couldn't seem to say it. His teeth clenched together until his jaw started to hurt. Like his body didn't want him to say no. A cry for help maybe, one he thought he should listen to. Life seemed to get worse every day at the Malloy ranch. He desperately needed to get away from home for a while, away from Cheshire and perhaps his nightmares. Being home brought him too close to them...too close to his past. The Bounty Ranch was a good twenty-five miles away, far enough to outrun his personal demons for a few days maybe. He didn't mind helping out with the building either. Working with wood calmed him like nothing else could.

Besides all that, he'd never refuse to help his baby sister.

"When do we leave?"

"Is today too soon?"

"You want to leave *today*? Didn't you come here to help Regina and Ray with the baby for another week at least?"

She grimaced. "Yeah, I did. But Regina basically threw me out already. Ray is too wrapped up in trying to take care of the baby to notice. And no one else in the household is going against her highness."

It was a situation the entire Malloy family did not like, but was helpless to stop. Ray had basically made his bed— particularly when said bed resulted in a baby—and he had to lie in it.

"I was kind of hoping the baby would mend their fences."

"Me, too, but I guess not."

They were both silent for a moment. Nicky gave him one more quick hug.

"You'd better take a bath, Jack. I'm not riding all day in a wagon with you when you smell like the wrong end of a horse."

"You don't like my skunky odor, eh?" he said, trying to be lighthearted for her.

"No, I surely don't. I'm going to go light the stove and make coffee. Come down when you're ready. I'll be waiting for you."

Jack knew what she meant. When he was ready to talk, she'd be ready to listen. This morning, she was going to be listening to silence because Jack wasn't talking. And he never would be.

Jack sat on the bed for hours, staring at the wall, wondering how the hell he was going to get through the next day, the next week, hell, the rest of his life. A dark cloud hung over him and he didn't know how to escape its shadow.

CHAPTER TWO

The cradle he'd made for Nicky's baby was strapped in the back of the wagon. He'd made it from rosewood, one of his favorites, with maple inlays. It was a beautiful cradle if he did say so himself. He was content, well, as content as he could be, when he worked with wood, whether with a hammer and nails or a knife to whittle. It was soothing. And nowadays, it was the only peace he found.

His gloved hands held the reins of the wagon as they traveled across the snow-covered ground toward the Calhoun homestead, called the Bounty Ranch. It had been a long, cold trip across the range in the middle of March. Even with blankets around them, they were both cold. And Nicky, damn her, could not sit still. He was about to stick her in the back of the wagon and make her stay there just so he didn't have to watch her.

Nicky groaned and bumped him with her dang big belly again.

"Are you sure you're all right?" Jack asked grudgingly as he watched her squirm on the seat for the hundredth time in the past hour.

Nicky ground her teeth and nearly growled at him. "I'm fine. It's only another mile or so."

"I just don't want your husband to take it out on me when you show up blue from the cold and in early labor."

Nicky's reply was a punch to his arm. "Ow!"

"My ass is sore, if you must know. I am not in labor."

Jack hid his grin and choked back the laugh that threatened to burst from his throat. Unbelievably, his arm was smarting from Nicky's sharp knuckles. Even pregnant, she was fierce enough to give a good measure of herself in a fight.

"Okay. Okay. I give up. Please don't hurt me, Mrs. Calhoun."

Her scowl started to turn into a grin, even as she fought against it. "Dammit, Jack, concentrate on driving this rig, not on my butt."

The laugh exploded from him like a rifle shot. After trying to frown at him, Nicky gave up and joined him.

"Jack, it's so good to hear you laugh again."

He frowned at her. "Would you just let me be, Nicky?" He hated that he sounded whiny, but dammit, she was worse than a dog with a bone.

"I'm sorry, Jack. I can't, and... Stop the wagon."

"What?"

"I said, stop the wagon."

Jack dutifully pulled back on the reins. "Whoa, boys, whoa." The horses nickered in the cold, their breath like vapor clouds around their heads. When the wagon stopped, Jack heard a horse, coming fast. He turned to the source of the sound and watched the rider approach them, his hand gliding to the pistol that rode on his right hip. Before he knew what was happening, Nicky had clambered down from the wagon and was running through the snow toward the rider. With the snow up to her knees, and seven months pregnant, hers was not an easy gait.

"Tyler," she yelled.

Jack rolled his eyes and pulled his hand away from the pistol. It was Nicky's husband. The two of them were so affectionate it made a person want to lose his breakfast, lunch and dinner. And maybe tomorrow's too.

* * * *

Tyler Calhoun saw his wife trying to run to him and he grinned. It was not so long ago that he never smiled, and now it seemed he couldn't stop whenever Nicky was around. Ten feet from her, he pulled Sable to a stop and dismounted in one motion. In three long strides, he reached his wife and picked her up like she weighed less than a feather. She squealed as he swung her around in a circle, laughter and love in her green eyes. Her nose and cheeks were red from the cold, making her look at least five years younger than her twenty-three years. She wrapped her arms around his neck and brought her cold lips to his with urgency. He groaned as their kiss grew hot enough to scald, and his cock woke up with a growl.

"Magpie," he whispered when their kiss broke. "I missed you."

She began to rain kisses all over his face. "Not as much as I missed you, bounty hunter."

"What are you doing home already?" he asked. "I thought you were going to help Regina for a month."

Nicky frowned. "She didn't want my help, so I left."

"Is that Jack?"

"Yes, it is. He looks terrible, Tyler. I am so worried about him and I don't think he's sleeping at all. I told him we needed help to finish the addition."

Tyler knew there was more to that story, but this wasn't the place for the discussion. Her lips were still wet from his kiss and he couldn't resist tasting them again. She moaned as his tongue entered her mouth.

Jack cleared his throat loudly as he approached in the wagon. "Do you think you could save that for later? My ass, as well as the rest of me, is about numb from the cold."

Tyler chuckled under his breath. Sometimes it didn't seem real that he had a wife who loved him, who was heavy with his child. Life had never been so good before he met the Malloys.

"Good to see you too, Jack," Tyler said as he carried Nicky back to the wagon.

Placing her beside her brother on the seat, he said, "Ride in the wagon, honey. You're too far along to risk riding on Sable."

"Yes, dear," she replied, still clinging to his neck.

Jack snorted. "What did you do to her? Cast a spell? If you did, you'd better share it with the rest of us."

Nicky turned and punched her brother in the arm again. "Ow! Dammit, Nicky, cut it out."

Tyler bit back a grin. "See you at the house, Malloy." He kissed his wife again. "Magpie."

* * * *

Nicky had nearly purred at Tyler when he pulled away. Jack was completely disgusted with the two of them. Jesus, he forgot how much Tyler and Nicky were like oversexed lovebirds. They were just so damn *happy*. It made his own misery that much deeper. He was rethinking the decision that would make him nauseous for the next two months.

Nicky watched Tyler return to his horse and swing up into the saddle, pride for her husband shining in her eyes.

"If you're done looking at your husband like a lovesick cow, can we get moving?"

She stuck her tongue out then smiled. "Lead on, brother dear, lead on."

Jack slapped the reins on the horses' rumps and they started on the last leg of their journey to the Bounty Ranch. And hopefully, towards a small respite from his nightmares, and some much needed sleep.

* * * *

Tyler had a surprise for Nicky. He was still grinning as he caught sight of the small ranch house. It wasn't much, but it was all theirs, purchased with their combined money. It had a kitchen and living room downstairs, and two bedrooms upstairs. Tyler was adding a bathing room, and a room for the baby on the back of the house. He didn't know how to go about decorating the new addition, so he'd asked for help from Nicky's best friend, Rebecca Connor.

Rebecca and Nicky had met under the direst circumstances four years before in the root cellar of Owen Hoffman's ranch. Rebecca had been sold as a white slave, along with her cousin and a young boy, to Hoffman, the man engaged to marry Nicky. Nicky and her twin brother Logan had rescued the three of them, but Logan, and Owen's brother, had been killed in the process. Nicky had been an outlaw for more than three years because of it, which led Tyler to accept Hoffman's offer to hunt her for the bounty. When he found her, sparks flew, and they ended up falling in love. Rebecca and her cousin, Belinda, helped Nicky clear her name last fall. Jack and Tyler had killed Owen Hoffman when he tried to take Nicky's life.

Now, Rebecca had secretly traveled from Nebraska to Wyoming to help Tyler. A professional seamstress, she had been busy sewing and measuring for the past week since she'd arrived. Tyler couldn't wait for Nicky and Jack to get there, just to see the expression on her face.

Tyler led Sable into the barn to unsaddle him. He wasn't going out again today with Nicky back. He smiled again as he thought of his wife in their featherbed tonight, then shifted uncomfortably at the inevitable erection in his jeans. Damn, he still couldn't even think about her without getting hard.

Noah was in the barn repairing some tack. The fifteen-year-old orphan used to work for Owen Hoffman. He was quiet, almost to the point of being painfully shy, and worked harder than any grown man could for Tyler. It had been Tyler who took Noah under his wing after Hoffman's death. Tyler already loved the kid like he was his own flesh and blood.

"Noah." Tyler smiled in greeting to the boy.

"Tyler," he replied.

"Nicky is on her way back so I need to get on into the house to warn Rebecca. We'll have a nice big supper tonight, so you be sure to wash up good," Tyler said as he walked Sable to his stall in the barn.

"Yes, sir...I mean, Tyler," Noah said, nodding.

Noah was a great kid. Any man would have been proud to call him son. He would have been astonished to know that Tyler and Nicky had talked about adopting him.

After giving Sable a brief rubdown and some oats, Tyler hastened to the house.

"Rebecca?" Tyler called.

"In here," came her voice from the kitchen.

He walked into the small room to find Rebecca cutting fabric on the kitchen table he'd made nearly six months ago for his growing family. It wasn't as good as something Jack could make, but it was sturdy. Now it seemed the table was growing into a mountain. There were sewing implements covering every square inch. He eyed the mess with a frown.

"What's the matter, Tyler?" Rebecca was a little bitty thing, just over five feet tall, with nearly white blonde hair and enormous gray eyes. She resembled a petite porcelain doll compared to his sensuous, tall wife. Rebecca was a beautiful woman, both inside and out. He had deep respect for her. She had a spine of steel and more courage than many men did.

"How can you keep track of everything in that pile of stuff?" He looked over all the materials with a bit of concern. How the hell was she going to clean all this up?

She smiled. "Don't worry, I know where everything is. I swear," she said as she held up a hand.

"All right." He still had a hint of doubt.

"Tyler, is something wrong?"

"What? Why?"

"You're here doing nothing in the middle of the afternoon."

Tyler could have slapped his forehead in self-disgust. "Shit."

It was Rebecca's turn to frown. "Please don't curse."

"Sorry, sorry." He paused, grinning. "My surprise is ruined, Rebecca. Nicky is on her way home right now."

"What?" Rebecca exclaimed. "Oh, no, I'm not even half done yet."

"It doesn't matter. Now you can spend a few more weeks with her."

"I hadn't thought of that. That is wonderful. When will she be here?"

Tyler glanced outside through the small window above the sink. "I'd say within the next ten minutes or so."

Rebecca's heart warmed. She had been thrilled at the prospect of visiting Nicky. When Tyler had proposed the surprise, she'd been more than eager to help out. Life in small-town Nebraska could get a bit boring, even with her cousin Belinda as company. Well, it wasn't really fair to call it boring, but something was definitely missing. Growing up, Rebecca had hoped for a husband and a family, as most young girls do. All of that, her hopes and her future, had been brutally stolen from her. Though now she had a good life, she wasn't truly happy or content. Truth be told, she was somewhat unhappy. Tyler's letter was like a sign from heaven that something had to change. And a chance to visit with Nicky when she was expecting her first child was the perfect opportunity to escape her everyday life and see her best friend at the same time.

Excited and unable to stand still, she went to the stove to put water on to boil for tea. Then she popped the leftover breakfast biscuits in the oven to warm up. Nicky was bound to be cold when she arrived and Rebecca wanted to be ready. As the water boiled, she meticulously cleaned up her sewing supplies. She prided herself on using only the best equipment, which included a sewing machine, safely tucked into the guest bedroom she occupied. Just as she finished piling the supplies, she heard the sound of a wagon outside.

Tyler popped his head back in the kitchen and looked like a little boy on Christmas morning. "Stay here," he told Rebecca, with mischief in his eyes. "I won't tell her a thing." He disappeared out the front door.

Rebecca chuckled at his boyishness. Until you gazed into his eyes, he looked more like the bounty hunter he used to be, with black hair, ice-blue eyes, standing at six foot four inches with over two hundred twenty pounds on him. Who'd have thought this huge, fierce ex-bounty hunter would be such a romantic for his wife?

She smoothed her skirt with both hands, then clasped them in front of her and waited for Nicky to enter.

* * * *

Tyler bounded outside to meet the wagon. With a swish of gray wool, he scooped Nicky into his arms.

"Hello, Mrs. Calhoun," he whispered in her ear.

"Hello, Mr. Calhoun," she responded a little breathlessly.

"I'll unload the cradle, then take the team to the barn," said Jack. "Don't worry about me."

Tyler and Nicky only had eyes for each other.

"Close your eyes, magpie," Tyler instructed as he carried her toward the house.

"Put me down." She frowned at him.

"Nothing doing. You can't walk with your eyes closed and pregnant, so I'm going to have to carry you," he said as one hand caressed the side of her breast. She gasped. Tyler grinned and waggled his eyebrows. "Now, close your eyes."

Nicky smiled and closed her eyes. Tyler brought her through the front door, and then closed it with a kick. When he reached the kitchen, he winked at Rebecca and set Nicky on her feet.

"Okay, you can open them."

* * * *

Jack was reaching for the second strap on the cradle when he heard Nicky yelling. Like a bullet out of a gun, he slammed into the house and ran into the kitchen, all but knocking Tyler aside.

"Nicky!" he shouted when he saw her being held down by someone. Pulling Nicky aside, he grabbed hold of one arm of her attacker and yanked unmercifully. The intruder crashed into his chest and looked up at him.

Jack was going to faint. Right there, right now, in front of all of them. The blood drained out of his face and puddled somewhere around his ankles. In his arms was the woman who haunted his nightmares, whose screams echoed in his dreams. The face of the petite blonde was burned into his brain like acid. Rebecca Connor. He made a croaking sound of dismay.

* * * *

Jack Malloy. A more handsome man she'd never seen. Wavy brown hair and beautiful cornflower-blue eyes. However, he didn't look his best at the moment. Rebecca grew concerned as she gazed at Jack. He was as pale as milk, his eyes were unfocused, and he was weaving on his feet.

"Mr. Malloy?" she said.

Jack jumped away from her as if boiling water had scalded him. Rebecca had to grab hold of the table so she didn't go tumbling to the floor.

Nicky and Tyler spoke at once.

"Jack, what the hell are you doing?"

"Rebecca, are you all right?"

"Fine. I'm fine," she replied, rubbing her arm where Jack had grabbed her. Lord, he was strong.

"John Gideon Malloy. What did you do that for?" Nicky turned on her brother.

"I...I thought Nicky was in trouble," said Jack as he caught sight of his brother-in-law's thunderous expression.

"And you didn't think I could handle it alone?" Tyler said.

"I don't know, Tyler. I'm sorry, I...I didn't think about what I was doing."

"You don't have to apologize to me, Jack. You need to apologize to Rebecca." Tyler crossed his arms over his chest and scowled.

Jack's gaze never left the floor beneath her feet. "I apologize, Miss Connor," he said stiffly.

She tried to be gracious. "Of course, Mr. Malloy. These things happen."

Jack mumbled something about the cradle and the horses and then fled the house with a slam of the front door. Nicky and Tyler looked at each other in surprise, then burst out laughing. Rebecca smiled as she thought of the incongruity of her attacking Nicky Calhoun.

"What was that all about?" asked Tyler.

Nicky shook her head at Tyler, and then slid a glance at Rebecca.

Rebecca wished she could one day share that silent communication with a partner, like Nicky and Tyler did. Not likely, but a girl could still wish.

* * * *

Jack carried in the cradle an hour later. It was covered in a tarp, piquing Rebecca's curiosity. Nicky had been so excited about it, going on and on about how beautiful it was until Tyler dragged her upstairs to rest. And Jack had made it. Apparently he had been the family's official furniture maker for at least the last ten years. It was hard to believe a fourteen or fifteen-year-old boy could make furniture that well. She'd been surprised to learn how many of the pieces in the Malloys' ranch house were actually made by him. Surprised and very impressed.

He brought the cradle into the addition and she followed him. Normally being in a room with a man was uncomfortable for her, but for some reason she hadn't felt that way with Jack. Perhaps because he seemed even more uncomfortable around her. Jack set it on the floor with care, then took the tarp off.

Rebecca was nearly rendered speechless. She had never seen such a beautiful piece of craftsmanship. The cradle was made of rosewood with lighter-colored inlays that were tiny little angels. The rockers were shaped and matched perfectly. The beauty of it was simply incredible. She walked over and he jumped to his feet. He resembled a deer staring at a hunter, wide-eyed and tense.

"I was wondering if I could touch it."

He continued to simply look at her.

"The cradle, Mr. Malloy. May I?"

He nodded, but did not relax his stance one smidge. What in the world?

She ran her hands along the wood. It was smooth and nearly seamless. "You made this?"

He seemed to find his voice. "Yeah, I did."

She gazed into his distrustful eyes and smiled her friendliest smile. "It's magnificent. You have a true talent, Mr. Malloy."

"Jack."

"I beg your pardon?" She wasn't sure he'd even spoken.

"Call me Jack. When I hear Mr. Malloy I turn around and look for my pa."

On a good day, he probably would have delivered that statement with some of his humor, which she'd heard about but hadn't witnessed yet. But today was apparently not a good day for him. He looked just horrible. His eyes were blood red, the rims swollen and he had huge dark circles under them. She could see his hands shaking. Cataloguing the symptoms in her head, as her father had taught her to do, Jack had either given up long-term drinking, or he had not slept in some time. She believed it was the latter.

"Very well, I will call you Jack, if you call me Rebecca."

He nodded.

"Thank you for letting me see the cradle," she said as she left the room. "It's a wonderful gift."

* * * *

Jack dropped down on the floor after she left.

Holy hell.

He had wondered what it would be like to see Rebecca again instead of dreaming her. On the one hand, she reminded him of the nightmares he was trying so desperately to forget. On the other hand, he felt a strange pull, an attraction to her. He'd sensed it before when they'd first met six months ago. It had frightened him then. It frightened him now. He tried to tell himself it was just pure lust. Possible, but not likely. It's not as if Jack hadn't felt pure lust around women before. It was more like he never followed that lust. He'd always resisted the pull.

The reasons why remained buried deep inside. With Rebecca it was definitely different.

Maybe it was because she was in his dreams. Granted they were not erotic dreams that men should be having about women, but still. She was there and always beautiful, always pleading with him for help. God, if only he could help himself.

He didn't know what the strange pull was. But when she ran her hands along that cradle, he had been astonished to feel himself harden. He imagined it was he she was caressing with those small, slender hands. He had to suppress a shudder of longing before she saw his body shake with need. There was *something* between them.

And he didn't know what to do about it.

So he decided to avoid her, to exit the room if she entered, to not even speak to her unless she spoke to him first. Self-preservation was a mighty strong thing to resist. He had a feeling that if he didn't run, he would never be the same. That scared the hell out of him.

CHAPTER THREE

Nicky had much to say to Tyler when they lay sated and deliciously nude in each other's arms, spooned together in their favorite snuggling position. She told him about her new niece, Melody, that her sister-in-law Regina had given birth to ten days ago in Cheshire. Regina and her husband, Nicky's brother Ray, had barely spoken two words to each other since the birth and the tension in their house was as thick as pea soup. Nicky tried to help her sister-in-law with the baby, but Regina adamantly refused. Ray hired an Indian woman to wet nurse the child because Regina refused to be part of such a "barbaric practice".

It was whispered, but not said straight out, that Melody was not Ray's daughter. He doted on her like any father would, though, more than Regina did for the poor little mite. All of the Malloys had brown, light brown, or reddish hair, and Regina was blonde. None of them had the shock of straight black hair Melody sported.

Nicky also told Tyler about her concern for Jack, and why she'd asked him to stay to help them finish the addition. Tyler agreed with her plan and was glad to have Jack's skilled hands.

"What do you think is bothering Jack?"

Nicky considered Tyler's question. "I don't know, but we need to find out. I tell you, the sound he was making in his sleep made the hairs on the back of my neck stand up at attention. It's soul-deep, whatever it is. And he looks just awful."

"Did you talk to the rest of your family about it?"

She nodded. "Ethan and Trevor both told me he was normal up until I came back." She paused. "Tyler, what if I *am* the reason?"

Tyler stroked her belly with his callused hand. "Impossible."

"But—"

"I said impossible." He squeezed her lightly then kissed the back of her neck. "Keep at him, magpie, he'll have to give in sooner or later."

"Maybe Rebecca can help pry it out of him." Nicky smiled in the darkness. "Who knows, maybe they'll end up liking each other."

"Don't play matchmaker, Nicole Francesca Malloy Calhoun. Do you hear me?"

Nicky didn't answer, and Tyler couldn't see the grin on her face. Perhaps Jack and Rebecca could end up liking each other after all. With a little help, that is.

* * * *

It wasn't as easy as Nicky thought to corner her brother. Jack could be as slippery as a greased hog when he wanted to be. Actually he seemed to be taking great pains to avoid everyone but the livestock; in fact, if she didn't know him better she'd swear he was *running* from her.

Three days after they got home, Nicky and Rebecca walked into the living room. She was astonished to see Jack closing the window behind him. She glared at him and tried to block Rebecca's view, embarrassed that her brother was going to such lengths to avoid her.

That doggone fool jumped out the window.

Obviously Nicky had to resort to Plan B. Rebecca.

* * * *

They were in the kitchen the next afternoon. Nicky folded the baby's freshly laundered diaper cloths while Rebecca sewed lace on the curtains for the new room. When Nicky suggested that Rebecca would be perfect to help her find out what was bothering Jack, she felt like she'd been poleaxed.

"Me?" Rebecca dropped the curtain she was sewing onto her lap. "You want *me* to find out what's bothering Jack? What could I possibly do? I mean, it's no secret that Jack has never liked me, Nicky. You can't say you don't notice it. I think I even saw him climb out the window yesterday when we came into the room."

"I don't think he'd go that far, but..." Nicky sighed. "The truth is, Rebecca, I'm desperately worried about Jack and I've run out of ideas. He isn't sleeping or eating, and he's in a foul mood half the time. Have you seen those dark circles under his eyes? Something is eating away at him like a poison, and I can't figure out what it is. You two have never really had a chance to get to know one another, so I thought maybe...perhaps..."

Rebecca closed her eyes and squeezed the bridge of her nose between her thumb and forefinger. She didn't think she'd be able to get even one civil word out of Jack Malloy, but Nicky was her best friend. She simply couldn't refuse.

"All right. I'll see what I can do."

"Thank you. Thank you. Thank you," Nicky crowed, jumping up to hug her friend.

Rebecca's heart twisted as the little Calhoun baby kicked her. Before she could catch herself, she jerked away from Nicky's stomach.

Nicky frowned at her. "What's wrong?"

"Nothing," she replied, hoping she looked like she was telling the truth. "How am I ever going to be alone with Jack long enough to talk to him? He's pretty scarce."

Nicky opened her mouth to speak, but Rebecca was saved from further scrutiny when Jack walked into the room. "Speak of the angels and they flap their wings," her mother used to say. Nicky greeted him affably. Rebecca was polite.

"Hello, Jack."

He was as irresistibly handsome as ever. His dark chocolate hat was pushed back on his head and his cheeks were pink from the cold. His sheepskin jacket was well-worn, but not as worn as those indecently tight jeans he wore. *Lord have mercy.* She could see the outline of his... But she shouldn't be looking there. It was definitely not appropriate. Luckily neither Jack nor Nicky noticed her wandering gaze.

Was it hot in the room?

"I, uh..." He apparently couldn't remember what he wanted. His bloodshot eyes darted between them.

He couldn't even look at her. And she was supposed to become his confidante? If anything, he looked like he'd rather hoof it to Texas than be in the room with her.

Nicky stared at him with one eyebrow raised. "Jack, did you want something?"

"Tyler."

Nicky rolled her eyes. "What does Tyler need? Should I get a slate and some chalk for you?"

He appeared embarrassed by Nicky's impatience. Rebecca saw her opportunity.

"Does Tyler need something from me? Needle and thread? A piece of scrap material?"

Jack almost seemed relieved. "Some scraps for hooves. One of the wagon horses got a pebble and is tender."

"Of course," she said as she went into the addition to dig through her material scraps. Jack followed her in. She had some dark blue flannel left from a shirt she'd made for Tyler for

Christmas. That would be perfect. She kneeled down to access the burlap bag she kept her scraps in.

"I know just the thing. Just give me a moment."

* * * *

Jack stared down at the halo of blonde hair and the blue wool dress that belled out like a flower beneath her. Rebecca was so different from what he expected. Not many would sit on the floor of a room covered in sawdust to retrieve scraps of material for a horse. And very few of them would do it without complaining. He watched as her little hands pulled out perfectly folded scraps of material, all different colors and sizes until she apparently found what she was looking for. He squatted down next to her.

"Aha!" She held up some dark blue material. "How many?"

She turned her face to his and those enormous eyes locked with his. My God, why had he followed her in here and why the hell was he so close to her? He felt like he had fallen on an ant pile—jittery, anxious, and annoyed at himself.

"Jack?"

"What?" Without intending to, he practically snapped at her.

"How many pieces does Tyler need?" she calmly repeated, although her cheeks were pink.

Jesus, why was he such an idiot around this woman?

"One—no, better make it two so he can double wrap it for him."

She handed him the material. And her hand *almost* touched his. He flinched at the near contact, then straightened and stomped out of the room, the material clutched in his hand.

* * * *

Well, that went swimmingly. He was rude, short, and curt with her and didn't even say thank you. The strange thing was, he looked embarrassed to be behaving like a boor. She didn't understand it. It was almost as if he couldn't help himself. What was it about her? Maybe she should just ask him.

Returning to the kitchen, she found Nicky snacking on a biscuit and staring out the window at Jack's retreating back.

"So, you were alone together. Anything?"

Rebecca sighed. "No, Nicky. He can barely stand me. I don't think I'm going to be able to even speak to him, much less find out his deepest secrets."

Nicky finished the biscuit and wiped her mouth with her arm. Some habits die hard, and living like a man for three years had apparently allowed Nicky to forget how to eat like a lady. Rebecca smiled at Nicky's sheepish expression.

"Well, at least I didn't burp really loud."

Rebecca laughed with her as they both took biscuits and Nicky sat at the table.

"How about some tea?"

"Sure."

Rebecca was pumping water into the pot when Tyler walked into the room with what appeared to be a telegram. He looked angry and frustrated.

"What is it?" Nicky asked.

He held up the paper. "James just brought this by with the rest of the wood for the addition. It's a telegram from your pa."

Rebecca knew it could not possibly be good news if Mr. Malloy sent a telegram.

Nicky snatched the telegram out of his hands and read. The emotions crossing her face ranged from disbelief to anger to sorrow.

"My God. Regina left Ray and the baby." Nicky scowled. "I have to go back to Cheshire. How dare she abandon a baby like that? Who could possibly do that?"

Rebecca swallowed, her throat as dry as the desert wind. Her stomach had somehow crawled up near her heart. "I can't imagine."

"My pa doesn't say much besides that. Well, I'll know more when I get back to my parents. This time I'll take Tyler with me."

Something akin to panic zipped through Rebecca. "What? You can't leave me here alone with Jack."

Nicky and Tyler both looked surprised at her outburst. "You won't be alone with Jack. Noah is always here, and at night both he and Jack sleep in bunks in the barn loft. You can lock the doors, Rebecca. You'll be safe."

Rebecca waved her hand. "I know I'll be safe. It's just, well, you know he doesn't like me, Nicky. I suppose I could catch leprosy and maybe then he might be okay with being in the same room with me."

"Leprosy? What in heck are you talking about?" Tyler asked.

"I don't know. I think I swallowed a stupid pill," Rebecca said, now really regretting giving in to Nicky's cajoling.

Nicky patted her shoulder. "Don't worry. You're such a nice person, Rebecca. Jack can't help but like you."

"Nicky," Tyler warned.

"Never mind," she said as she steered him out of the kitchen. "Let's go pack. I want to leave tomorrow morning."

She turned and mouthed "thank you" at Rebecca.

Rebecca sighed as she shook her head slowly back and forth. "A fool's errand for a fool like me," she mumbled. Setting aside the sewing, she stood and stretched her back, getting the kinks out of her muscles.

* * * *

Jack had seen Tyler talking to the man from town, and then he walked back to the house, clutching a piece of paper. Jack set the material on the upturned bucket near the horse's stall and followed his brother-in-law to the house. When he got there, he went immediately to the kitchen, then stopped in the doorway.

Well, hell.

He watched, no, not just watched. His eyes ravenously devoured Rebecca's body as she stretched her small frame, thrusting her breasts forward. The soft light from the oil lamp created a halo around her blonde hair. She had a perfect figure, a perfect face, and an unforgettable past.

Jesus H. Christ. Run!

He must have made some kind of sound, because Rebecca yelped in surprise and grabbed her scissors. She turned and held them out like a weapon, her eyes wide with fear. Jack was completely taken aback. He'd never expected someone like Rebecca to take a defensive posture with a pair of scissors. She was so damn small and dainty-looking. Now she looked pretty lethal with a sharp weapon.

"Jack!" she exclaimed as she lowered the scissors and took a deep breath, dropping her gaze to the table. "I'm sorry. I seem to keep startling both of us, don't I?"

Jack didn't miss the trembling in Rebecca's hand or the frantic beating of the pulse at the base of her neck. He hadn't stopped to consider how she reacted to men after her experience four years ago as a white slave. It's no wonder she didn't take his head off before she realized who he was.

"You don't need to say you're sorry, Miss Con—I mean, Rebecca. I scared you again," he murmured, shifting from foot to foot. "I'm sorry." He adjusted his hat on his head and turned to leave.

"Jack." Her hesitant voice stopped him. "Can you stay a

moment? I need to speak with you."

Jack weighed the possibility that Nicky had set him up for Rebecca's probing skills, but dismissed the notion. She wouldn't be that devious. He leaned against the doorframe and fixed his wary gaze on Rebecca. His instincts were clawing at his backside, trying to get him to turn tail.

"Nicky got a telegram today from your father," she began. "Apparently your sister-in-law has left Raymond."

Jack's mouth thinned to a tight, angry line. "That goddamned bitch," he mumbled under his breath.

"What did you say?" she asked with her head tilted, tawny eyebrows drawn together.

"Nothing you want to hear," he grumbled. "Damn that woman, anyway."

"Please don't curse."

He ignored her. "How the hell could she take Melody away from Ray?"

Rebecca shook her head. "She left the baby behind." She spoke as softly as a summer breeze.

"What? She abandoned her own child? How could she do that? That heartless bitch. I guarantee I know where she went— San Francisco. If I leave now, I can probably catch up with her—"

Rebecca shook her head again. "Jack, you need to wait and talk with Nicky. She and Tyler are going to your parents' ranch to help sort things out."

"Oh. So I guess that means I'm stuck here."

"I guess so."

"Are you going with them?"

"No."

"Oh," Jack said again.

He considered the implications of that and didn't like it one damn bit. He walked quickly—he was *not* running—out of the kitchen. It was going to be damn hard to avoid Rebecca now.

* * * *

Tyler, of course, asked him to stay at the ranch to keep an eye on Noah and Rebecca, as well as all the animals. Jack could not refuse. There was no reason on earth for him to refuse, except for his own unceasing cowardice. It wasn't something to admit to a large, fearless brother-in-law.

The next morning, Nicky and Tyler left amidst a flurry of hugs from the expectant mother. They promised to be back within two weeks.

Two weeks yawned like a bottomless pit to Jack. Two weeks alone with Rebecca Connor—the woman who didn't, and couldn't, know that she haunted his dreams. She looked innocent enough, almost blindingly beautiful, and Jack knew he was inexcusably rude to her. He couldn't seem to help it, no matter how polite or distant he tried to be. Something inevitably popped out of his mouth that was entirely inappropriate, and most times brought color to Rebecca's cheeks, whether in anger or embarrassment. He waited to eat breakfast until he was absolutely sure she wouldn't still be in the kitchen. His stomach complained loudly about the delay, but Jack ignored its bellows. Well, for Pete's sake, it was past ten o'clock.

He opened the front door to the house and stamped the snow off his boots onto the rag rug. After closing the door behind him, he pulled off his gloves and hat and hung them with his coat on the wall hooks beside the door. He listened for a moment to the silence in the house. He'd never realized how much noise Nicky made, he thought with a grin.

Stepping into the deserted kitchen, Jack spied apples in a bowl on the table and was reaching for a particularly juicy-looking one when a voice stopped him.

"There's a plate for you in the oven."

Damn.

"I'm not really hungry," Jack mumbled as he snatched the apple. To his mortification, his stomach picked that moment to yowl. He glanced at Rebecca. She was standing in front of the doorway to the addition with white curtains draped over her left shoulder, and a pincushion in her hand.

"All right," she said with a raised eyebrow and a small grin playing around her lips. "Well, if you want it, it's in there. Biscuits, bacon and eggs."

Jack's stomach rumbled louder. Rebecca laughed, then slapped her hand over her mouth to stifle it. He realized he'd never heard her laugh in the six months he'd known her. Her laugh was musical, and definitely did something to Jack's equilibrium. He stared at her, a little bewildered.

"I apologize, Jack," she said. "I shouldn't have laughed at you."

Jack shook his head. "No, it's okay. I was just surprised to hear you laugh, I mean, you haven't, well, at least I haven't heard you... Well, you surely don't need to apologize."

Why do I even bother opening my mouth only to put my foot in it?

"Well, I'm glad to be friends with someone who can make me laugh." She paused. "We are friends, aren't we?"

No, I can't.

"Any friend of Nicky's..." he began, then took a huge bite of his apple and avoided her gaze.

"Jack, I don't mean to be rude, but is there something about me that you don't like?" She looked so seriously at him that Jack felt like a complete horse's ass.

"No, there's nothing wrong with you."

High praise indeed. Must make her feel all warm and loved.

"I'm going to be honest with you, Jack," she continued, glancing down and fingering the lace-trimmed curtains. "I don't think you like me, and I just wanted to know why. Is it because of what happened to Logan? Because he died saving my life?"

Jack gulped. How was he supposed to answer that? It was so far from the truth, it was almost funny. Jack didn't know what to say so he simply said nothing.

Setting the curtains on the back of a chair, Rebecca took a cloth to pull his plate out of the oven, then put the plate on the table. Taking an empty cup, she filled it with hot coffee from a pot on the stove and placed it in front of the plate with a fork and knife.

"Eat, please," she murmured. Retrieving the curtains from the back of the chair, she retreated through the open doorway with grace, dignity, and a hint of lavender.

Jack swallowed his disgust at his actions. He couldn't let her go on believing he didn't like her because of something that wasn't her fault. Hell, he could hardly keep from imagining how soft her lips must be at the same time he was gauging how far away the front door was. His brain was all twisted up like a bramble bush. Grabbing his breakfast, he followed her through the doorway.

* * * *

Trying to ignore the hurt from Jack's dismissal and obvious dislike, Rebecca held up the curtains to the window in the new room. There was quite a bit of work to do, and the rest of the furniture to be completed, but at least the curtains were nearly done. Standing on her tiptoes, she stretched herself to her limit, but still could not reach the top of the window to properly check the length on the curtains.

"Darn it," she mumbled.

"I think I've been a bad influence on you."

Jack's deep voice startled her so badly she must have jumped a foot off the ground. "Lord above, Jack. You scared me to death."

Jack turned to go back into the kitchen. "Sorry about that."

Rebecca grabbed his arm and stopped his retreat. "Oh, no, you don't. You can earn that breakfast by holding these curtains up to the top of the window so I can measure."

Touching him felt like a spark off a burning log—hot, sizzling and definitely uncomfortable. She almost jumped out of her skin from the sensation. At the same time, it was incredibly exotic to touch a man and not feel fear, but rather excitement. Jack set his plate on a stool and took the curtains from her hands, which were thankfully not shaking.

"It's a good thing all you Malloy men are tall," Rebecca mused as she watched Jack hold the curtain up to the top of the window without even really stretching. "I'd have to strap buckets to my feet to reach all the way up there."

Jack looked like he was trying not to grin. He glanced out the window.

"It's snowing."

Rebecca was surprised to see the small, white flakes fluttering to the ground. She hadn't expected it to snow, and she was sure neither had Nicky and Tyler.

"Do you think they'll be all right?" she asked.

"Probably. They're headed southeast so they should be ahead of the storm. Besides, it's just starting. They ought to get to the ranch in about four more hours. It probably won't amount to much anyway."

"I hope you're right."

As he held the curtains up above the window, she kneeled down to pin the bottom. It was an awkward position for her and he seemed to be dancing in place, like he needed to visit the necessary or something.

"It'll just be a minute or two."

"No problem," he said, and yet he didn't stop moving. He was like a little kid in church.

"Am I keeping you from something?"

"Just breakfast."

Oh, right. She'd forgotten about his breakfast sitting there on the stool. It would get cold quickly so she put the pins in as fast as she could, jabbing her finger twice. The second one went pretty deep and she yelped.

"Are you okay?"

She looked up, way, way up to Jack's face. From the floor, he appeared to be a giant. All of a sudden, she felt dizzy and Jack's face wavered a bit, becoming another face, another man, another time. She dropped the pins on the floor and scooted backwards so fast she got a splinter in her hand. The feeling of panic almost overwhelmed her. Jack seemed to sense her fear because he didn't move a muscle, even at her odd reaction.

"Are you okay?" he repeated.

Grateful for his consideration, and embarrassed by her behavior, Rebecca nodded and rose from the floor with as much grace as she could muster, then walked back over to the window.

"I'm sorry. I don't know why I did that. Sometimes my mind plays tricks on me, I think." She reached for the curtains.

He looked at her gravely as he laid the curtains on her outstretched arm. "You don't need to apologize. I understand."

Meeting his gaze, she knew, just *knew*, he meant what he said. He understood about minds playing tricks, about being afraid. Without asking, he kneeled down and picked up all the pins she had dropped then put them in the tin on the floor. Straightening, he took his breakfast in hand and went back into the kitchen alone.

There was a heck of a lot more to Jack Malloy than the sweet, gentle man Nicky always spoke of and the odd, jittery man who took pains to avoid her. Much more. The question was, did she want to find out who he really was?

CHAPTER FOUR

The gentle snowfall turned into a howling, full-blown blizzard. The shrieking sound of the wind had an eerie human-like quality that crawled up Rebecca's back like an unwanted insect. She didn't like it one bit. Being trapped in the house without being able to go outside was maddening. She had to keep busy. So she sewed until she thought she'd go blind, and then she cooked while Jack and Noah shoveled the path to the barn. At least they had been able to go outside—not that being out in a blizzard was pleasant—but it was still outdoors.

Rebecca made beef stew and biscuits for supper. She kept glancing out the window as the darkness closed in on the whiteness beyond.

"Foolish men," she muttered as she put the bowls and plates on the table with a little less care than she should. *Thunk.* "Staying outside until their toes turn blue and drop off." *Thunk.* "Makes a body worry to death about them." *Thunk.*

The front door banged open with a gust of icy cold air and a whirl of fat snowflakes. Two snow-covered figures stumbled into the room and slammed the door shut behind them.

"Becky," breathed the larger one. "Help Noah. He's nearly frozen through."

Who the heck was Becky?

Rebecca was nonplussed for a moment. Shaking her head to clear her surprise, she moved to the smaller figure's side. She hooked one arm around his waist and walked him to the crackling fire. The ice and snow from his clothes wet her dress through, but she hardly noticed.

"Easy now, Noah," she murmured. "Let's get you out of these wet things."

As she removed Noah's ice-encrusted jacket, she felt Jack's eyes on her. Rebecca dropped the jacket on the floor and started to unwrap Noah's scarf. His nose was as red as a radish. She heard Jack removing his own sodden jacket, which landed with a thump and a tinkle of ice on the wooden floor. The snap of a suspender made her jump. Just the thought of Jack undressing behind her made her stomach do a little jig. She hoped he wouldn't get naked. Or did she? Her confusion turned her anger on.

"What possessed you to keep this boy out in a blizzard for two hours?" she hissed at Jack over her shoulder.

"Necessity. We'll have to go back out and shovel again in a while. If we don't, we'll have a helluva time getting to the barn so the animals don't starve, and the cow's udder doesn't explode."

"Please don't curse," she said without even thinking about it.

She sat Noah on the couch and tugged at his boot, but it didn't budge an inch. "Did your feet grow while you were outside?"

Noah laughed. She tugged harder until it popped off and she landed on the floor flat on her backside. She grinned at him and got back to her feet.

"Now that was stuck on pretty good. Let's hope the other one comes off easier."

* * * *

Jack watched Rebecca take care of Noah. She performed each task without complaint, even when she landed on her perfect little ass on the floor. Nicky would have been screeching at the top of her lungs. It was getting harder and harder not to like Becky, even as he was trying to pretend she wasn't there. In fact, it was impossible. Becky—he couldn't think of her as the Rebecca of his nightmares anymore—had broken down his self-imposed wall of silence by just being herself—a kind, funny, warm person. A person who didn't deserve his ill treatment. Shame crept up his neck at the thought of how many times he had ducked around corners and even crawled out a window to avoid her. Maybe getting to know her better would keep her from his dreams. He could justify that all day, but the truth was he wanted to be with her more than he wanted to avoid her.

"Perhaps we should work in shifts then. I'll take the next one."

Jack's eyebrows shot up as far as they would go. Rebecca planned on taking a shift shoveling?

"No, I don't think so," he said.

"Since you're neither my husband nor my father, you have no authority over me, Jack Malloy. I *will* take a turn shoveling. I grew up in Michigan and I live in Nebraska. I'm not inexperienced when it comes to snowy weather." Her schoolmarm voice made Jack smile inwardly until she stood up with her fists planted on her hips. Her damp dress was plastered to her body, molding to her curvy outline. Lord above, this woman had a figure like a Greek goddess he'd seen in a book. The snow and ice started melting off Jack like a stream as his temperature rose ten degrees. And his pants were suddenly *very* snug.

"I'm going to get some dry clothes for both of you from Tyler's things. I know they won't fit, but they'll be warm and dry," she continued, patting Noah's shivering shoulder. "And you'll have to spend the night here as well. No sense trying to shovel your way to a cold barn when there's more than enough room in the house." She marched from the room with her spine stiff and purpose in her eyes.

Noah glanced up at Jack with wide eyes. "She's like an army general or something."

Jack grinned. "Do you think I can convince her to stay in the house?"

Noah shook his head. "Not a chance."

"That's what I thought, too."

* * * *

That woman must be part mule. No matter what Jack said, Becky either ignored him or changed the subject. Her middle name was Stubborn. She had put on a pair of Nicky's jeans under her dress. When she came down the stairs, she nearly fell on her head because the jeans were way too long. Now she was perched on a kitchen chair, trying to roll the legs up enough so she didn't trip on them again.

"Nicky sure does have long legs," he commented.

She didn't even blink. "Practicality is more important than fashion at this point, Jack."

"Hell, I know that, Becky. It's just that I don't know many women, besides my sister, who would want to shovel at all, much less with jeans over their drawers."

"Please don't curse," she said as she colored prettily.

"You know you have to tie a rope around your waist to shovel. Men have gotten lost between the barn and the house in a blizzard."

She still didn't miss a beat. "I'm aware of that. I fully planned on tying off to the porch before I started shoveling."

She picked up the first boot, which was nearly as big as she was. He watched her stuff rags in the toes so they wouldn't go flying off her feet. The boots were apparently some Noah had outgrown. At this rate, she'd be going outside in minutes. He had to stop her. No manner of man would let a little bit of a woman do a man's job.

Since she wouldn't listen to words, he had to go into action. She was tying the laces on the first boot when he made his move. Snatching up the other boot, he stood back and waited.

"Give me the boot, Mr. Malloy."

"No."

"You will give me the boot now."

"No."

Looking up at him, she sighed with barely concealed impatience. She held out one hand while tapping her fingers against her knee with the other. He ignored all of it. After all, he was the man in charge.

"What makes you think I cannot handle shoveling snow? I told you, I grew up in Michigan and have lived in Nebraska for the past four years. I know what snow is and I have shoveled acres full of it. Now, give me the boot."

"No."

She bent her head, untied her boot, then pulled out the rags. Jack grinned gleefully. He had won that battle; now if only he didn't feel like a team of horses had used him for kicking practice. Turning to walk into the living room, he rubbed the small of his back and had to close his eyes against the pain. Shoveling snow was not the kindest taskmaster.

A sudden draft of cold air slapped his face. He opened his eyes to find the door closing behind Becky. She'd gone outside anyway. Damn stubborn woman.

She was wearing *his* boots.

Well, hell.

* * * *

Rebecca shoveled for an hour. The snow was relentless, but so was she. She kept at it and got at least ten feet done on her own. Probably a lot less than the men could have done, but that was ten feet of snow Jack and Noah didn't have to shovel. She was quite proud of herself.

When she finally came in, shivering and so grateful for the warmth of the house, Jack looked mad enough to spit nails, but all he did was glare at her. Still, that was marginally better than ignoring her or embarrassing her, which was all he'd managed to do until now. She changed into dry clothes and had a hot cup of tea to warm up. The shoveling wasn't that bad—well, it was, actually—but it wasn't unbearable. She could live with it for an hour at a time.

It was nearly midnight when she had a chance to sit and relax on the living-room sofa. Noah was in bed and Jack was, amazingly enough, sitting on the floor, propped against the other end of the sofa, whittling. Normally he'd have hightailed it for the barn as soon as one of her feet stepped into the room. He looked a little nervous, kept darting glances her way now and then, but he was there, in the room, with her.

Wonders never cease.

Rebecca was embroidering a blanket for the baby. It was yellow fleece with green and blue flowers. Blue like the color of Jack's eyes. Her mind was definitely wandering if she thought about his eyes when working on a baby's blanket. Usually sewing and embroidering were her escape, something that brought her peace and kept her grounded. Tonight, she felt jumpy instead. Perhaps it was because Jack was there. And he was so big; the room seemed to be half its size when he was in it. She watched his back, the way his muscles moved and bunched as he worked on his craft. And for some reason, she kept remembering how tightly his jeans molded to his body.

It was definitely warm in the room. Almost too warm.

Jack was concentrating on his whittling. She tried to look, without appearing like she was looking, at what he was carving. It seemed he was paring off the most minute shavings from the little figure. They were so tiny she could barely see them. And she couldn't see what the figure was because his hands were too big. Long, strong fingers and big palms. Oh, my.

"What is it?"

He started at the sound of her voice, nicking his thumb with the small but lethally sharp blade. She belatedly realized she had just blurted out her question.

"Oh, Jack, I'm sorry." She pulled her handkerchief out of her pocket and sat on the floor beside him. He moved away from her ever so slightly and sucked at his thumb. His gaze looked her over. She tried not to flinch at the withdrawal or the perusal.

"You'll get your dress dirty," he said around his thumb.

She shrugged. "It's not as if it's satin or taffeta, Jack. It's just wool."

After he grunted at her response and continued to stare at her, she sighed and started to rise. When he laid his hand on her arm to stop her, it felt like a branding iron. Hot. She had to grit her teeth to block the flinch from escaping—a flinch of pleasure and excitement.

"Please don't go. I'm sorry. I can't... I reckon I don't act proper when I'm around you... I... Well, never mind why. Don't go." The words tumbled out of Jack's mouth.

He stuck his hand out for her examination. She was surprised to see what appeared to be a hint of fear in his eyes.

Why in the world would *he* be afraid of *her*?

When she took his callused palm in her hand, the feeling was incredible. She sucked in a breath of surprise. A rush of peace, of rightness, wound its way through her, just from touching Jack. She looked in his eyes and didn't see fear anymore. She saw wonder and puzzlement. Perhaps her touch elicited peace as well. How peculiar.

She averted her gaze to his thumb and examined the cut. It was still damp from Jack's mouth. To her embarrassment, she had the urge to put her own mouth on his thumb. That was enough to make her wiggle on the floor. Pushing away her odd and somewhat lascivious thoughts, she concentrated on his wound. It was superficial, not very deep at all. The bleeding had almost stopped. She dabbed at it with her handkerchief. The nearness of him, the warmth of him and the fire, made her want to cuddle up and sleep with him by her side. Naked.

Good Lord.

"It's an angel," he said.

She blinked. "What's an angel?"

He held up the little figure he'd been carving. Sure enough, it was a tiny angel with wings unfurled. The detail was so vivid she could almost see the individual feathers. He could do that without even trying?

"Jack," she said. "You have got to be the most talented woodworker I've ever seen. You're an artist."

He turned the angel to look at it. "It's just whittling."

"No, it's more than that. I saw the cradle, the pieces at your parents' house, and now this. I tell you, you are an artist."

"Well, being an artist doesn't keep your belly full, Becky."

She wanted to convince him of his talent. "But you could, in a large town or city, sell your work, your furniture, and easily make more than enough to money to feed you. You are so gifted."

He peered at the angel again and frowned. "Nah. I'll stick to horses and cattle. It's safer."

"It's your life, of course. You're still very good in my opinion, Jack. More than good. Your work is the best I've ever seen."

She couldn't tell in the firelight, but she'd swear he blushed.

He cleared his throat, his gaze never leaving the wooden figure in his hand. "This was supposed to be a toy horse for the baby. When I started carving it...it just decided to be an angel instead. A couple more nips and it'll be done."

He looked down at his hand clasped in hers. She was mortified to discover that she was still holding his hand. The blood had stopped, but she hadn't let go. Deep down, she decided it was because she wanted to keep touching him, to keep that *peace* flowing through her. She dabbed at the cut one more time as if just finishing, then let him go.

"There you are. Good as new. I don't think you'll need a bandage," she said, trying to sound brisk instead of like a hussy in heat.

He pulled his hand back carefully. "Much obliged, Becky."

She didn't get up. Sitting next to him was too comfortable, too enticing to move.

He went back to his whittling. She watched, fascinated, as he turned it this way and that, examining it before using the knife to remove the tiniest shaving.

After five minutes, he put the knife back in its scabbard on his hip. He scrutinized the angel once again then abruptly held it out to her. She took it and noted it was warm from his hands. Peering at the angel's tiny face, she thought it looked...well, actually, a little like her. Absurd. He didn't even like her.

"It's amazing. The detail on the wings is...well, it's so real. I can even see the individual lines in the feathers."

He glanced at the figure again. "I don't set out for it to be like that. It just sort of...happens."

She nodded. "Yes, it's like that for me when I'm embroidering. I have a picture in my head, but it just..."

"Happens." They both said at once.

Smiling, she held it out for him to take back, but he shook his head.

"Keep it."

She shook her head. "I can't. This is too lovely to accept."

He looked at the angel in her hand. "I've been a real horse's a—er, behind around you, Becky. Consider it a peace offering."

Peace.

She opened her mouth to refuse again, but he laid two fingers across her lips to stop her. Her lips twitched with the absurd urge to kiss his callused fingers. A flare of heat moved through his eyes as he slowly lowered his hand.

"You'll hurt my tender feelings if you say no." He smiled.

It was the first time he'd ever smiled at her. And oh, sweet Mary and all the heavenly saints, it was a *beautiful* smile. The sincerity in his eyes and that smile silenced any objections. She curled her hand around the little angel, her gift.

"Thank you, Jack."

"You're welcome."

They sat in front of the fire together. Not reading, or sewing, or whittling. Just sitting and talking. Rebecca was content—no, more than that, almost happy. She also felt drowsy. She leaned toward the sofa to rest her eyes.

* * * *

It had started out as an experiment. He had wanted to see how long he could stay in the room with her without running or flinching or acting like a complete jackass. And it was working. When she sat next to him, it had been difficult not to get up and run. But then she'd touched his hands and something had happened. He couldn't explain it if somebody had asked, but it was as if a river's current started flowing between them. A current full of...well, it sounded corny and stupid, but peace and happiness. As if touching her were like touching all that was good in the world. Even when she released his hands, the feeling lingered between them, as if being close to each other made the current continue flowing. He wanted to sit next to her, wanted to be with her.

The experiment forgotten, they talked of their day, of the blizzard, of how hard Noah tried to keep up with Jack and Tyler. They were getting to know one another. And for the first time in a long time, Jack wasn't scared.

* * * *

The sound of the wind woke him. Jack opened his eyes and couldn't remember where he was. He squinted at the embers of a fire in front of him while the gray light of dawn crept through the windows. He was sitting on the floor in the living room and his left shoulder was full of pins and needles. He rubbed his eyes to clear the sleep out and when he looked down, he nearly jumped to his feet.

It was *Becky.* Asleep on his shoulder. How had *that* happened?

He remembered most of it. He remembered her beautiful gray eyes in the firelight. How she had nursed his thumb; at one point he thought she was going to lick it. That had sent a painful zing to his groin.

He remembered the pleasure and awe in her eyes as he showed her the angel. It had pleased him so much he gave her the angel. He hadn't meant it for her, but giving it to her was right. So right. It was almost as if he had carved it for her. If he was being honest with himself, the angel did resemble her a bit. Somehow.

He also remembered touching her hands and how there was such a strong pull, a feeling of rightness, between them. It was that feeling that had lulled him to sleep. Sleep.

Holy ever-loving Christ.

It was dawn. And he had slept. *Slept.* At least five hours of pure, uninterrupted, blissful sleep. Something he hadn't done in months. And all because he'd been next to Becky.

His nightmares had featured her for months, but here he was actually with her and her presence somehow kept the nightmares away. If that wasn't a kick in the nuggets. They weren't kidding when they said God worked in mysterious ways.

He turned and lifted her sleeping form into his arms. So small, she felt like a sack of feathers, but this particular sack of feathers had curves. Delicious curves. The weight of one sweet breast rested lightly on his arm. And Becky wore no corset. He was astonished to find himself getting hard from having a woman in his arms. Not just any woman though. This was Rebecca Connor. The woman of his dreams who could keep his nightmares away.

He laid her on the sofa and covered her with an afghan. She sighed lightly and curled onto her side. It made him want to carry her upstairs to her bed and lay down next to her.

Now that thought was shocking. Jack had never slept with a woman in his life. However, he knew, deep down in his heart, he would never have nightmares if he was with her.

* * * *

It had been another incredibly long day in a blizzard that seemed to like the Bounty Ranch so much it didn't want to leave. For the third time that day, or possibly the fourth, Rebecca was out shoveling. She would have boiled in oil before admitting it to Jack, but she had lost all feeling in her feet. However she would not fail at her task. She understood the importance of keeping the path shoveled to the animals. Rebecca didn't even want to contemplate what would happen to them if the humans entrusted with their care decided that numb feet were more important. And she refused to allow Jack and Noah to do all the work when she could contribute, too.

Her back was screaming and her arms felt like jelly. And beneath all the layers, she was sweating. Yes, sweating, not perspiring like a lady. She was sweating like a pig. And, unfortunately, she also smelled like one. Wafts of hot, fragrant air drifted up to her nose with every shovelful. It was *not* a pleasant scent.

Her nose had long since given up the battle to find a handkerchief and simply ran until it froze on her face. She knew she looked even worse than she felt. But it didn't matter. Nobody was going to get close enough to care.

In a split second, between the shovel up and shovel down, it was taken out of her hands. She fell forward with her body's momentum, heading straight for the icy ground. It felt like a tree limb stopped her descent. But it wasn't a tree limb. It was an arm, a strong arm, attached to an equally strong, *hard* body pressed against her.

"Whoa there, Becky. Don't decorate the snow with a bloody nose," came Jack's voice at her ear.

A shiver that had nothing to do with the cold traveled through her body.

"You're freezing," he said.

As she put her feet down and straightened, his arm slipped away. The loss was palpable, and she didn't even stop to contemplate why. She knew why. There was something between them and it was growing.

"Being out in a snowstorm for an hour can make even the heartiest soul long for a fire and a warm blanket, Mr. Malloy," she managed to squeeze out, hating how breathless she sounded.

"Back to 'Mister' are we?" he murmured. "I thought we moved past that."

Rubbing her blistered, mittened hands together, she finally turned to face Jack. He, of course, looked wonderful. Lord above, but his looks alone could make her knees wobble.

"Now, why did you take the shovel?"

He smiled. "Look up."

Rebecca was surprised to see the stars. Night had fallen and it had finally, thankfully, amazingly stopped snowing. She smiled back at Jack.

"Well, Hallelujah!" she exclaimed. She threw her hands up in the air and twirled, slipping on an icy patch. Jack caught her again, this time in his arms. His smile disappeared and his gaze zeroed in on her mouth. The silence of the cold night was as deep as the snow. He slowly, ever so slowly, lowered his head toward hers.

Holy crow, he's going to kiss me.

The first touch of his lips was cold, but in an instant, it was hot. Boiling hot. Stunned, Rebecca kissed him back. Her heart stuttered madly and she could hardly breathe. He moved his mouth over hers in a gentle caress. After a moment of infinite time, he pulled back.

He shuddered. "God, I am so sorry."

Rebecca blinked but couldn't yet make her voice work. Removing his arms from her like she was a breakable piece of china, he stepped back. Her body cried out from the loss. Nothing had ever felt so *right* as being in Jack's arms.

He ran a hand down his face. "I can't believe I just did that. I never..." He looked at his feet. She recognized his habit when he didn't want to say something.

"We'd better get inside where it's warm," he said, his voice strained.

She cocked her head and looked at him.

"Jesus Christ, Becky. Say something. God, I am sorry. You can't imagine how much."

She licked her lips and tasted the licorice drop he'd apparently been eating, and him, his essence. All that was Jack. Sorry?

"I'm not sorry."

Walking past him, she made her way back to the house, her head high and her back straight. It had been, after all, her first "real" kiss from a man. And it had been wonderful.

Sorry? Not bloody likely.

CHAPTER FIVE

Jack's hands were shaking. Hell, his whole body was shaking.

Goddamn.

What had just happened? He had called to Becky, but she was a million miles away and didn't seem to hear him. A shoveling machine is what she looked like. He'd had to take the shovel from her. She had laughed and smiled to discover it had stopped snowing.

And then...

And then he'd done the unthinkable. He'd kissed her and held her beautiful body against his. Dammit all to hell, he had loved every second of it. In fact, he was throbbing with the need to do more. He grabbed a handful of snow and pressed it against his burning face. What he ought to do is shove it down his pants to wilt the incredible hard-on he was trying unsuccessfully to will away.

What the hell had happened? It was as if for a moment, he forgot everything but her. There was only that moment, that one perfect moment. Her lips had felt softer than rose petals, and she kissed like it was her first kiss. Being with her was turning his life into a dream instead of a nightmare. A wonderful, erotic dream.

"Jack!"

Noah's shout broke Jack's reverie with a start. Here he was out in the freezing cold mooning over a stolen kiss.

"Jack!"

Noah's voice was sharp. Noah was never sharp. Something was wrong. He turned and ran toward the house and all but threw the shovel when he reached the front porch. Noah was standing in the light thrown by the open door, coatless, hugging his thin body with his equally thin arms. The worry was clear in his eyes.

"What is it?"

"Miss Becky." His voice was almost a whisper. "When she took the boots off, I saw her crying, real silent-like. I ain't never seen her cry about anything afore."

"The boots?"

Noah nodded. "So I asked her if'n anything was wrong. She wiped the tears to pretend like they wasn't there and smiled at me. But it weren't a real smile."

"*And?*" He felt like shaking the boy to hear the rest, or clapping his hand over his mouth so he couldn't hear it.

"She said she was fine. A blister or somethin'. But when she tried to stand up, she fell down on the floor and really started crying."

Jack pushed past Noah into the house, shedding his outer layers as he ran for the living room. What he saw almost made *him* cry.

Becky was lying on the floor in a fetal position. Great big tears streamed down her face. Her grimace of pain almost made Jack want to run back outside. Almost.

"Becky?" he said gently as he slipped off his wet boots and hunkered down beside her. "Becky, honey, what's the matter?"

She turned her face toward her shoulder. Jack picked her up and set her on his lap on the sofa. Stroking her back, he tried not to let his distress show. Here was one of the strongest women he knew reduced to a pile of tears and pity. He pulled his neckerchief off and wiped her cheeks with it.

"You know tears will make your eyes red and your nose run. At least it will when your nose defrosts," Jack teased, trying desperately not to panic.

"Jack," she whispered. "They hurt. Oh, God, they hurt so much."

"What hurts?"

"My feet."

Her voice was so low he almost didn't hear her.

"They were numb, but I thought it was just from the cold. Just from being out in the snow. But when I started to warm up by the fire, it felt like hot pokers on them. Oh, sweet Jesus, I couldn't even stand on them. Jack, it hurts so much."

"Will you let me help you?" Jack's hands hovered over her feet.

Will you let me touch you?

She didn't hesitate. "Yes, please, help me."

She sounded so small, so wounded. Jack had to swallow the lump in his throat before he could speak.

"Noah, get some warm water. Not hot and not cold, just warm, and a blanket, towel, and some dry socks." He was proud his voice didn't shake.

Noah was off like a shot. Jack heard the boy banging around in the kitchen as he retrieved the warm water from the reservoir on the stove.

Standing up slowly, Jack laid her on the sofa and put a pillow behind her head.

"Hang on, Becky, I need to take a look at your feet. It's going to hurt a bit, but I'll try my damnedest to be gentle. Okay?"

She nodded. "Please don't curse."

Grimacing, he ignored her remark and handed her the neckerchief.

"Be brave for Dr. Jack and I'll give you a licorice drop."

One corner of her mouth lifted.

"Good girl."

The socks were frozen stiff with ice, the tips of them slightly damp from the fire's warmth. Jack slid her rolled-up pant legs a little bit further up. When he reached the tops of the socks, he slowly, gently began to roll them down. Her calves were the color of ivory and incredibly soft. Biting the inside of his cheek to focus, Jack continued. He saw bright red skin, just above her ankles. A small whimper stopped him. He glanced up, and didn't continue until she nodded again. After the bright red of her ankles, the tops of her feet were white, not ivory. White like snow, like frostbite. That's when he discovered the socks were literally frozen to her feet.

"Noah! Where the hell is that water?"

Noah came rushing in with a bucket, sloshing a good portion of it on the floor and himself as he strained against the weight. "Here. Here it is."

Jack took the bucket from him and set it on the floor by the sofa. He met Becky's pain-filled gaze.

"I've got to turn you so I can put your feet in the water, darling. Do you understand?"

The tears hadn't stopped flowing, but she didn't make another sound. She continued to only nod.

"Did you make these socks?" Anything to keep her mind off the pain. "I wasn't sure if you worked with yarn, too."

"No, that's Belinda. She knits and crochets like a tornado," she said softly, her words ending on a gasp.

Tasting blood from his cheek as he desperately tried not to hurt her, Jack swung her legs over. He stuck a finger in the water to test the temperature.

"Towel," he barked.

Noah handed him a towel that Jack set on the floor by the bucket. Cupping her left calf in his hand, he lowered it into the warm water. He glanced at Becky. Her face was pinched, pasty white, and her eyes were closed. And she had the little wooden angel clutched in her hands. His heart missed a beat.

"You're doing fine, darling. Let's get these frozen critters off your feet. Belinda might have to make you another pair."

As the warm water began to melt the sock from her foot, it seemed to Jack that a layer of her skin was peeling along with the wool sock.

"Almost got the first one off." He concentrated on getting the goddamn socks off instead of the damage he was doing to her beautiful feet.

Becky released a long shuddering breath and wiped her cheeks.

"I'm sorry I'm hurting you, sweetheart."

She shook her head quickly. After he got the sock off, he set her foot completely in the water and handed the sodden sock to Noah. He repeated the process with her right foot.

"We're going to warm your feet up real slowly," he said, massaging her calves to get the blood circulating.

She nodded again.

"You know for a woman with a tongue as sharp as a hunting knife, you're awfully quiet."

She tried to smile. Jack wanted to absorb her pain through his hands. Touching her no longer evoked any kind of fear in him. He thought if he *couldn't* touch her, he'd go crazy.

* * * *

It was truly heaven and hell. Jack's hands were so gentle, the water soothing, and his voice comforting. But her feet felt like a thousand shards of glass were stuck in them. It was excruciating pain, the worst she'd felt in a very long time. Only their connection, the peace that flowed between them, kept her from sobbing uncontrollably.

"If you have pain, it's good," Jack said.

She knew her eyes were as wide as saucers. What was good about it?

"It means the frostbite didn't take hold yet. It means you won't lose your feet."

"Oh."

Jack smiled at her. "I knew the chatterbox would return."

It was too hard to smile back at him on the outside, so she kept it behind her eyes instead.

"Thank you, Jack."

He averted his gaze quickly and stood, drying his hands on the towel. "Let's get some hot food into you."

Jack went into the kitchen to join Noah and left her alone. She heard their low voices, but couldn't catch what was said.

A moment later Noah, looking like a scared rabbit, came in carrying a steaming mug.

"Miss Rebecca?" he said. "Jack said to bring you this coffee. I know you don't cotton to it—I told him so, but he said he didn't give a sh—I mean, darn. Um, he put whiskey in it too."

He handed her the mug with a beet-red face.

"Thank you, Noah. It's all right. Jack is just trying to warm me up inside and out."

He shuffled his feet. "You scared the bejesus outta me when you fell on the floor. Are you gonna be okay?"

She forced a brightness into her voice she desperately was not feeling. "I'll be fine."

He looked as if he didn't quite believe her, but he nodded and went back in the kitchen.

Jack came next with a steaming pot of water. If she wasn't in so much pain, she might enjoy two males waiting on her. What woman would have ever expected to experience that?

"I need to warm up the water a bit. Don't worry, I won't scald you."

He tipped the pot and trickled hot water into the bucket. Forget the thousand shards of glass; she felt the full force of two thousand shards now. She sucked in a breath and tried to concentrate on Jack instead and not scalding herself with the hot coffee in her shaking hands. She hadn't known he could be so concerned, particularly for her. But that was definitely concern, if not outright worry, in his eyes.

"You're very kind, Jack. I can see it's a family trait."

He glanced up at her. "I haven't been kind to you before now. In fact, I was a downright jackass. I'm sorry for that."

"Nothing to be sorry for. We can start over. Hello, it's nice to meet you." She held out a hand. "I'm Rebecca, I mean Becky, Connor."

Jack set the pot on the hearth, then turned and shook her hand briefly. His callused hand felt like a hot mitt around hers. A jolt went through her arm straight to her heart. "Pleased to meet you. John, I mean Jackass, Malloy. But you can call me Jack."

She laughed. Jack was charming, utterly enchanting.

"Now drink my godawful coffee and whiskey."

He laid the blanket on her and made sure she was comfortable. When he tucked a strand of hair behind her ear, they both froze. Something passed between them, a pulse of pure energy.

As he removed his hand, his thumb lightly brushed her cheek. She didn't think it was an accident. Time stood still again. Her pulse grew stronger; the sound of her thumping heart flooded her ears. Jack leaned down toward her. A tingle raced right up from her toes to her head...could this be desire?

He's going to kiss me again.

Their second kiss was a bit like the first. The touch of his lips on hers sent a distinct jolt through her entire body. It was like lightning bugs had landed on her mouth. His lips moved over hers slowly, but she wanted more.

"Angel," he breathed against her lips.

"More."

He deepened the kiss, slowly licking his way from one end of her lips to the other. His tongue was a little rough and the feel of it on her lips was enough to make her want to dive into him like a pond on a hot day. Then his tongue entered her mouth and she wanted *more*.

"Jack," came Noah's voice from the kitchen.

Jack wrenched his lips away and leaned his forehead against hers, breathing heavily. She sucked in a much needed breath.

"That boy has great timing," he growled under his breath.

This time Becky reached up and touched his stubbled cheek. "I am very pleased to finally meet you, Jack."

Jack closed his eyes and seemed to tremble just a bit under her touch.

"Jack. I need help out here."

He pulled back to return to the kitchen.

"We'll need to continue this discussion...later," she said.

He smiled and ran his thumb over her lower lip. His blue eyes had become so dark, they looked almost black.

"Later."

Becky watched his back as he walked away. God sure did know what He was doing when He made a man like Jack Malloy.

* * * *

Jack cooked dinner. Well, it was sort of a dinner. Warmed up beans, slightly overdone bacon, and something that resembled biscuits, but were a mite chewy to really be considered biscuits.

Noah brought her the food. He also added more hot water to the bucket. And Jack...Jack seemed to be hiding in the kitchen. Becky decided she didn't want to play the ignore game anymore. When Noah came in to retrieve her dishes, she said, "Noah, please ask Jack to come in here."

He nodded and scurried back to the kitchen. Jack poked his head in the room a few moments later.

"Did you need something?"

She saw a flash of discomfort and a smattering of guilt in his beautiful eyes.

"Yes. Please remove my feet from this bucket. It's been long enough. I'm a little waterlogged and the pain has faded to a dull roar."

Jack frowned, but stepped into the room. *That's more like it.* She pretended not to notice the flour on his shirt, or the bacon grease fingerprints smeared on his pants.

"Are you sure?"

"Yes, very sure. I also need to, ah...use the necessary."

Twin spots of color appeared on Jack's cheeks. When was the last time she saw a man really blush?

"Hell, Becky, I'm sorry. I don't know why I hadn't thought of that."

After she reminded him, again, not to curse, Jack lifted her left foot from the water. He carefully examined each toe, every nook and cranny. Her foot was pink, not white, and throbbed less insistently than before. He used the towel to pat her foot dry, and then took the right foot out for careful examination.

After both feet were dry, he began to put a dry wool sock on her foot as if dressing a newborn babe.

"Jack?"

"Hm?"

"I'm not an infant."

He looked up at her with confusion plain on his face. "What?"

"I'm a woman grown. The way you're putting that sock on, I thought perhaps you mistook me for a baby."

His eyes darkened again and the pupils seemed to grow wider. "You can be sure I know you're a woman, Miss Connor."

The sexy timbre of his voice was unmistakable. She trembled under his gaze. So *this* was desire. Passion. And it had lurked inside her for six months. Since the first time they'd met and the spark flared between them. She hadn't thought herself capable.

"'Miss'? I thought we were past that." She almost didn't recognize her own voice.

The room felt decidedly too hot. She longed to rip off the wool sock and the blanket to cool off her heated body.

As Jack rolled up the sock completely, the caress of his hands sent sparks up her legs. The tingling was so vivid she could practically see the sparks. He repeated his gentle care with her other foot. By the time he was ready to pull her jeans legs back down, she was butter on a hot skillet. No wonder people were naked when they made love. It was too darn hot to keep any clothes on. She reached down and stopped his hand before he could touch her jeans.

"I need to take those off."

Jack's eyes widened and she actually *heard* him gulp.

"It's too warm. It's uh...very warm in here."

He started to speak, but nothing came out. Instead he only nodded, and picked up the towel and bucket to return to the kitchen. Becky was astonished to see Jack's male member clearly outlined in his jeans, clearly hard, and clearly quite large.

Oh my.

Touching my feet did that?

Becky grinned to herself as she shimmied the pants off under her skirt.

CHAPTER SIX

Jack practically dropped the bucket on the floor. He vaguely noted the water splashing on his feet.

How the hell did he go from avoiding and ignoring her to nearly tossing her skirt up on the sofa? It was bad enough that he'd kissed her. Twice. He used to shake with fear around her; now he shook with hunger, with rampant desire. He wanted her. Wanted to sheathe himself in her hot, wet core.

Just thinking about her soft feet and calves had the blood rushing even faster to his painful erection. He'd probably faint from loss of blood to his brain. He crossed to the sink and pumped the handle for some cold water. A *lot* of really cold water. Heedless of his dry clothes, Jack stuck his whole head under the icy stream. He yelped with surprise.

"Jack, are you all right?" came Becky's voice from the other room.

Blotting his hair on a towel, he answered, "Just fine." Okay, it was more like a squeaky croak, but he did manage to answer.

"As soon as I can tear the tent down in my pants, I'll be fine," he mumbled under his breath.

"I've taken the jeans off. It's safe to come back in."

Safe?

Jack groaned. The tent refused to come down. If anything, the tent pole was rising and the circus was coming to town. His damn cock had taken over his body.

Toweling off his hair, he went into the living room. There she was, lying on the sofa, her feet up on a pillow.

She looked at him and blinked. "Why are you all wet?"

"I slipped."

Her eyebrows shot up in surprise, and what he thought was disbelief.

"I'm going to go check on the animals. Will you be okay in here by yourself?"

She nodded. "Of course. Thank you, Jack. For everything."

When she smiled at him, he cursed his tight pants and left the room as quickly as possible.

＊ ＊ ＊ ＊

Jack carried her upstairs to her bedroom that night. It felt very odd, like she was a pretend bride and he a pretend groom. His cheeks were a bit pink when he set her down, whether from exertion or something else, she couldn't say. When he asked her if she needed help with anything else, she wanted to tell him, *Yes. Undress me.*

When had she become so wanton? Being around Jack had opened a spout that had been closed off all her life. But now it was flowing, and she was along for the ride. Loving every second of being with him, touching him, wanting him.

He slept outside the bedroom on the floor. Becky didn't ask why. When she woke in the morning and called him, he was there in an instant, looking sleep-tousled and incredibly sexy. He had slept though, something she suspected he'd been having trouble with for some time. The symptoms of sleep deprivation she'd noticed on the first day had begun to fade a bit. She wasn't about to question him about sleep or where he did it. She was content knowing he slept, and seeing him first thing in the morning set off a firestorm of vivid imaginings. It didn't help that his shirt was half-unbuttoned and she could see his chest. It was tanned and smooth, with very little hair. She actually curled her hands into fists so she didn't reach out and stroke that chest.

She was definitely a wanton. She didn't know how it had happened, or why it was only for Jack. But she was and it was only for him. There had never been any other man who had conjured up thoughts like this from her. It was almost magical, like a spell had been cast over her. Over them. She saw the looks Jack gave her from underneath those eyebrows. The heat alone from his gaze could singe her hair.

Being trapped in a house in a Wyoming blizzard with him was just making the net of the spell that much tighter. And they were getting closer every day. Soon, the net would tighten around them and there would be no escape. Except in each other's arms.

For a full day, Jack nursed her feet. They felt almost normal again, but he insisted she stay off them. It was a nice feeling really, to be cared for instead of caring for someone else. It also gave her an excuse to have Jack touch her. And oh, she really wanted him to touch her. Again and again. It was very addictive.

* * * *

After he'd carried Becky downstairs to the living room and given her some breakfast, Jack was drinking coffee at the kitchen table, trying to sort out his feelings for her. Hell, every time he got near her, he got an erection. It didn't help matters any that her eyes looked at him like he was a slice of apple pie she wanted to savor. It just made it that much harder to be around her—in fact, it made *him* that much harder. He was surprised he could think at all with the amount of blood that kept rushing to his crotch.

He was still amazed that being near her helped him sleep. Hell, he'd had more sleep in two nights than he'd had in the previous two months. He was glad she hadn't questioned why he was sleeping outside her bedroom. He'd be embarrassed to admit the reason.

The front door burst open and Noah came skidding into the room, bringing a rush of cold air and snow.

"Jack, it's Ophelia. I think she's gonna foal."

Jack frowned. The mare wasn't due for at least six weeks. Nicky would be devastated if anything happened to her horse.

"I'm coming, Noah. Let me tell Becky."

He ran into the living room as Noah ran back out the front door. Becky looked concerned when she saw the expression on his face.

"What's wrong?"

"I've got to go out to the barn. Noah says Nicky's mare is getting ready to foal. I didn't want you to be worried if I wasn't here."

"I'll be fine. I'm a tough girl, Jack. Is there anything I can do to help?"

Jack grabbed the image of her at that moment and burned it into his brain. Her on the sofa, hair slightly mussed, shoes off, cheeks warmed from the fire.

Heaven. *Peace.*

"Just pray."

With that he grabbed his coat and ran out the door.

* * * *

Becky dozed on the sofa. The fire was almost down to embers when she woke to see someone crouched in front of the fireplace. A well-placed poker jab had sparks flaring.

"Jack?" Becky murmured.

"No, ma'am, it's Noah. Jack sent me in to check on you. I'm sorry I woke you up."

She waved a hand in dismissal. "Don't worry about that. How is the mare?"

Noah was silent for a moment. "The foal was born dead, Miss Rebecca."

She gasped. "Oh, Noah, that's just awful. What is Jack doing?"

"He's cleaning up Ophelia. She ain't helping none either. Won't even stand up. It's like she wants to die too."

Tears stung Becky's eyes. She knew when a mother lost a child, she wanted to die too. It was only natural. That poor horse. And poor Jack.

"How long has he been out there?"

"About six hours."

"That man doesn't have the sense God gave a goose. It's below freezing outside and he's in an unheated barn for six hours? Did he send you in to keep warm?" She was furious with Jack. Did he not have a lick of common sense?

"Yes'm."

"How many times?" she asked in a steely voice, tapping her fingers firmly on the couch.

"Every hour."

"And has *he* come in at all? Even once?"

"No, ma'am."

Swinging her feet to the floor, she made a decision. And that was that.

"Noah, please get my boots."

"Ma'am, you ain't got no boots."

"It's 'You don't have any boots', and yes I do. Well, I mean the ones I was wearing before."

Noah looked like he was about to run for the door and keep going. His eyes widened and he opened his mouth to speak.

"*Now*, young man."

The steel in her voice worked its magic. His mouth snapped shut with an audible click and he went to fetch the boots.

* * * *

Hers was a slow pace but, due to Jack's expert care of her frozen feet, not painful. It was uncomfortable, and something she didn't want to think about later, but acceptable. Jack needed help and a good wallop on his backside.

Leaning on Noah's arm, she had just reached the barn when she heard Jack's soft murmuring. Her whole body clenched in recognition and sudden intense longing to be the recipient of that murmuring again. To feel the magic his care evoked. That was the voice he'd used with her when he had tended her feet. She swallowed hard. This was definitely not the time.

When Noah opened the barn door, the sight that met Rebecca's eyes nearly made her turn around and run back to the house to hide under the bed. This was going to be much harder than she thought. Blood was everywhere.

* * * *

Jack heard the barn door open, but he didn't look up from Ophelia. She was trying to die, and he was fighting for her to live. He couldn't explain the absolute urgency of it, but he had to save this horse.

"I know it's cold, girl, but you can do it. I put this warm blanket on you and that warm water we washed you with was nice, too. You can do it, girl. Come on," he coaxed, tugging at her head to force her into standing, but the mare wouldn't move. And he certainly couldn't make a one thousand pound animal move if she didn't want to. He was so exhausted his hands shook, and so cold he thought he'd never feel his ass again. But he huffed out a breath and bent down to try once more when he heard Becky's voice. His gaze snapped to her so fast, he saw stars.

"John Gideon Malloy. If you don't have the sense to come in from the cold, then in the absence of your mother and sister, the duty falls to me to make you warm up. What were you thinking staying out here so long?"

Her hands were fisted on her hips, her brows were drawn together and her lips were clamped into a thin white line. He almost expected her to tap her foot.

Her foot?

He stood up quickly while his knees screamed, but he ignored them in favor of his anger.

"What in the hell are you doing out here on your feet?" he yelled. "I spent the better part of a day nursing those nearly frostbitten feet and you're walking out here in the cold that damaged them in the first place?"

If possible, her frown grew deeper.

"We're not talking about me. We're talking about a senseless ox of a man who has been in a barn for six hours in below freezing temperatures."

She hobbled over to him and stuck her chin in the air. He half-expected her to smack him in the nose with it.

"You," she poked a finger at his chest, "need a bath and some warm food."

"I can't do that yet. And why the hell are you out here on your feet, dammit?" he snarled.

Jesus, please us, he didn't think he'd ever snarled in his life.

"Don't curse at me, Mr. Malloy. I won't have it. Noah, assist me, please." Although she hadn't raised her voice, he felt chastised anyway.

As he watched, she laid a folded blanket on the floor. Noah steadied her arm while she kneeled down and stroked the mare's neck. She spoke quietly into the animal's ear, which began to twitch. Her voice was low enough that Jack couldn't quite make out the words, but he didn't need to. The tone was so soothing, so empathetic, he found himself leaning toward her. Toward the comfort she was passing out. Out of the corner of his eye, he saw Noah do the same.

"Sweet, sweet Ophelia," he heard her say. "You must live. That beautiful baby wouldn't have wanted its mother to die. Let's get you up so the stubborn, handsome man can go inside."

Handsome? She thought he was handsome?

Her soft urging was apparently all that was needed. Ophelia raised her head and stood up with Becky. The horse's powerful muscles shook as she regained her feet. Then to Jack's astonishment, she seemed to lay her great head on the petite woman's shoulder and cry. He'd never seen a horse cry, but he'd bet every dollar he owned that Ophelia was crying. Becky's eyes closed and a tear escaped from beneath her lid to snake its way down her perfect cheek.

He swallowed a lump in his throat. Damn, that was amazing. How the hell did she do that? Was it a female thing? He ought to be furious that after three hours of urging, the horse hadn't budged, but after three minutes with Becky, she stood on her own. After a few more minutes of Becky's ministrations, Ophelia lifted her head and shook her mane.

"Good girl," Becky murmured. "Noah, escort her to her stall please. Make sure she's warm."

"Yes, ma'am," Noah replied, voice none too steady. Jack glanced at the kid's face and saw something that made him want to groan. Adoration, infatuation, puppy love. Now that was a complication he didn't want to deal with.

Becky stood for a moment with her hands clasped and her head bent. Jack didn't say a word, didn't want to spoil the moment. She let out a long, shaky breath, and then turned to Jack.

"Time to go inside, Mr. Malloy." Her voice was clipped and downright bossy.

"How did you do that? I mean, with the horse?"

"Sometimes a grieving mother needs the support of another grieving mo—woman."

Mother? Was she going to say mother?

"I see you tried to change the subject." The little foot really did start tapping this time.

"I can't leave the, um..." he jerked his head toward a blanket-wrapped bundle in the back of the barn, "...foal out here. The scent of blood will bring some coyotes or maybe a cougar."

When her eyes fastened on the blanket, her face turned white as a sheet. But she stuck that chin up again and he could see her will exerting itself.

"Yes, of course. Let's take care of the poor thing."

She hobbled toward the back of the barn. Jack followed her. Angry, elated, annoyed, excited, and fascinated with this little blonde woman. Yup, his fear of her was completely gone; now he was afraid of how deeply he was falling for her.

* * * *

The ground was too frozen to bury the foal, so Jack took stones from the pile behind the barn and brought them about twenty yards away. Rebecca didn't want to think the pile had been gathered for that express purpose. He shoveled a makeshift path to the burial site, and then brought the blanket-wrapped bundle. She walked behind him saying a prayer under her breath for the foal and its mother. Losing a baby, for any reason, was the worst kind of heartache a female, human or horse, could endure. This reminded her of her own pain, her own shame, and her soul-damaging decision three years ago. It still hurt so much it could snatch her breath away. She couldn't let Jack know how distressed she was, though. He must *never* know what she did. The shame would be too great.

After he laid the bundle on the snow, Jack went back to the barn for a moment.

"I'm sorry, baby," she whispered, hastily wiping frozen tears as Jack returned with a rifle.

"Can't be too careful," he said.

Setting the rifle down, he used the shovel to clear a larger patch in the snow, then picked up the foal and gently laid it down again.

He looked up at her as he started to pile the rocks in a circle around the blanket-wrapped bundle. "Did you want to say anything?"

She shook her head. "I said a prayer for it already."

That seemed to satisfy him, as he nodded and continued to pile the stones around it, making an oval-shaped pyramid of sorts. Leave it to a man to know how to pile stones together as a grave.

In a split second, she found herself violently shoved from behind, face first into the snow. An inhuman scream split the cold night air followed by a rifle shot. Rebecca cautiously moved her head and tried to regain the breath that had been knocked from her.

"Becky?" came Jack's horrified voice. "Oh my God. Becky?"

His hands turned her over in the snow. She blinked up at him as he wiped the snow from her cheeks. She was finally able to suck in gulps of the frigid air.

"Are you okay? Did she hurt you? Say something, dammit."

"Please don't curse," she whispered.

He tried to smile, but failed. "Goddamn cougar. I'm sorry. I should've been more on my guard. Those big cats are hungry this time of year. She was after the foal and squashed you like a flapjack." He cradled her face in his hands. "Sweet Jesus, are you hurt?"

She mentally surveyed her body. "No, just winded I think." She sat up with Jack's assistance. He started to brush the snow off her back and stopped suddenly. He uttered a curse she had only heard once in her life, and it made the hairs on the back of her neck stand up.

"What is it?" she asked with no small alarm in her voice.

He pulled her to him and hugged her tightly. The sensation of being in Jack's arms again was incredible. She could feel the frantic thumping of his heart beating against hers. And he was so warm.

"Thank God you're okay," he whispered. He moved back slowly and his eyes reflected many emotions, not the least of which was worry. Then he lowered his mouth to hers in a bruising kiss that managed to steal the breath she'd just regained. But oh, for such a different reason. His lips were strong, not insistent. His tongue roughly invaded her mouth and she was lost. Utterly lost. Twining her arms around his neck, she moaned and pushed herself closer to him. His grip tightened as the kiss grew deeper, hungrier. It was as if she were caught in a whirlpool, spinning faster and faster. Her breasts were tight, her nipples hard nubs that she ground into his chest. Wanting to be even closer, wanting much more.

"House, let's go. House," he gasped out.

Rebecca was about to agree heartily when Jack was ripped from her arms. The scream of another cougar singed her ears. A huge, tawny cat landed on Jack, toppling him to the snowy ground. They landed with a thud, then the cat attacked in earnest. It bit and clawed at Jack mercilessly as blood stained the snow beneath them. Jack was punching the cat and screaming curses. He struggled beneath its weight, trying to throw the cat off him, but its teeth had sunk into his shoulder like an anchor. Becky watched in horror as Jack battled for his life.

With a surge of anger, Becky screamed and shouted his name. She scrambled backwards, searching frantically for the rifle. It was lying on the ground beside the grappling man and beast. The slurping, growling noises the cougar was making were quite possibly the worst sounds she'd ever heard. Jack was still cursing and grunting as the snow turned even redder with blood.

"Leave him alone, you bastard!" she bit out as she aimed and squeezed the trigger. The shot went wild, pinging off a boulder. But it was enough to distract the cat. It let go of Jack and screamed again with a gust of warm breath in the cold night. The haunting bellow echoed in the stillness. Its golden eyes locked with hers and time seemed to slow to a crawl. Becky had been close to death before, but never stared it in the face. She now knew that her instinct was to fight. She wasn't about to give up while she could still help Jack. It lunged for her with Jack's blood dripping from its mouth.

Becky cocked the gun again. This time, God must have been guiding her hand because her aim was true. The big cat was felled by the second shot, sliding the last two feet to land in front of her. She was breathing hard, gulping air like a small child drinking cold milk on a hot day. She was also shaking so badly the rifle dropped from her hands into the snow.

"Jack!" Rebecca cried, running to his side. Kneeling down, she willed herself to not be sick at the sight of so much blood. Too much blood. "Can you hear me?"

She ignored the tears streaming down her cheeks as she looked into his glazed eyes. "Please, Jack. Say something."

Noah came running toward them from the barn.

"Noah, help me get him into the house. He's bleeding so badly."

Jack smiled at her. "You are so beautiful, Becky. Like an angel."

"Don't speak of angels, Jack. It scares me and I really don't need to be any more frightened that I am at this moment," she said, grabbing his hand and pressing the palm to her lips.

His eyes began to close. "My angel."

"Jack, dammit, don't you die on me."

CHAPTER SEVEN

Rebecca vaguely realized she'd cursed more in the past five minutes than she had in her entire life.

Jack was not a small man to move. No matter how hard they tugged, he only seemed to move a few inches forward.

"We need to make a litter so one of the horses can pull him to the house," she said. Holding onto her sanity by a slim thread, she sent Noah into the barn for blankets, rope and some wood for a litter. She knelt by Jack's bleeding body and started ripping the bottom of her dress into bandages. She pressed snow into the wounds, then wound the makeshift bandages around the worst ones. And she prayed. Prayed that they'd be able to stop the bleeding when they got him into the house, not *if*—that was something she refused to contemplate—but *when*.

"I'll be right back, Jack. Right back. Don't you even think about leaving."

She ran to the barn, ignoring the cold air on her now bare legs. She grabbed a bridle from the tack on the wall and put it on Sable, Tyler's horse. Leading the gelding out into the snow, she pulled him as fast as she dared. Noah was already back, putting the litter together with remarkable efficiency for a fifteen-year-old boy. In no time at all, he poked holes in the blanket with his knife, threaded the rope through, and tied it all together on two pieces of wood from the barn. Then he made an efficient loop to attach to the horse's reins.

"Are you ready?" he asked as he crouched by Jack.

She nodded and positioned herself on Jack's other side, opposite Noah. With a great heave-ho and another few curses— she'd better stop scolding Jack—they got him on the litter. Noah led the horse to the house, while she ran ahead to get the water boiling, clean bandages and her needle and thread.

* * * *

They set him on a blanket on the living-room floor and pushed the sofa back. Rebecca worked like a machine. She had to or she would lose her mind. Jack had lost copious amounts of blood, thanks in part to their inability to get him to the house quickly. He had deep claw marks on his chest and shoulders, both arms and hands were bitten, and there was one deep gash on his cheek, deep enough that she could almost see his teeth. She thought she was strong, but that one wound on his cheek nearly undid her.

Sweet Mother Mary. Help me be strong.

She packed new snow around the deepest wounds to keep the bleeding slow, but she didn't want to endanger him further by bringing his body temperature down. It was a delicate dance. Noah was working as hard as she was. He brought fresh snow, hot water, towels, cloths, bandages, whiskey to clean everything and needle and thread to stitch.

Rebecca felt like she was climbing a mountain made of loose dirt. As long as she held on, she wouldn't fall, but if she tried to climb, she slid backwards and had to start again.

She talked to Jack as she worked, mainly so she wouldn't go stark raving mad.

"I've got the left side stitched up. Nicky isn't going to be happy we tore up her sheets. We'll have to go into town and get some new material. I'll make her a new set in no time."

She tied off the bandage on his left hand. Looking at the bloody snow-packed bandages on the right, she covered her mouth with her hand to hold back a sob.

"Miss Becky?" She realized Jack had Noah calling her Becky, too. "Why don't you take your coat off? You're going to get powerful hot."

Rebecca nodded and slipped off the bloodied thing. She'd never wear it again. It was soaked with Jack's blood, his life. If anything happened to him, just the sight of the coat would... But no, he was *not* going to die. She was going to save him. She had to.

"Burn it, Noah." She handed the coat to him.

"You probably won't be able to fix those rips in it anyway," he said as he looked the coat over.

Rebecca turned and blotted her cheeks on her sleeve. "What rips?"

Noah showed her the back of the coat. From the top of the shoulders to the waist were long, savage rips the female cougar had torn when she had used her like a stepping stone. Swallowing hard, she remembered Jack brushing off her coat, and then stopping suddenly. That's when he'd started kissing her. If not for those damn rips, he'd have had the rifle ready and wouldn't be fighting for his life with an inept seamstress as his nurse.

This time she couldn't stifle the sob. Jack couldn't die because of her. Turning to her patient, she grimly went back to work. It seemed like hours that she cleaned, stitched, and bandaged his battered body. She was careful to use the tiniest stitches she could on Jack's face. He was so handsome a scar would only lend itself to his appeal. He'd probably swagger more now. And he certainly didn't need any other reason to swagger. He was perfect already. She tied off the end of the thread and snipped it. She gently laid a bandage on his cheek to protect the wound.

Done. At last. Done.

"Miss Becky?"

She started a bit at Noah's voice.

"Are you 'bout finished?"

She stood, or rather, tried to stand. Her legs were full of pins and needles and her back felt like it must be a hundred years old.

"Yes. We need to keep him warm and change the dressings in a few hours. We also need to get some water and broth into him."

"Anything else?"

As much as she didn't look forward to it, he couldn't stay on the floor. It was too cold and drafty.

"We need to get him upstairs into bed."

"The litter?" he asked with a wince.

"Yes, only this time, you and I are going to be the horse."

* * * *

They ended up securing a plank to the bottom of the litter to make the trip up the stairs less painful on Jack. They strapped him on with rope. She cringed a bit about having to do that, but at least there was a blanket between him and the rough hemp. She was afraid he'd fall off if he weren't secured. With Rebecca pushing and Noah pulling with all his one hundred twenty pounds, they yanked, dragged, winced, strained, and groaned Jack up the stairs one godforsaken step at a time. She knew if they stopped, they would never get going again, so she kept on, encouraging the young man she felt blessed having there to help her. Without Noah, Jack surely would have died. Rebecca simply would not have been able to save him on her own.

When they finally got to the top of the stairs, they slid the litter into the bedroom, ignoring the scratches they made in the floor. The cause far outweighed the result. Panting and sweating, Rebecca and Noah looked at the bed, then looked at the man lying helpless and unconscious on the handmade litter on the floor. It seemed like a long way up.

"Why don't we tilt up the end with his head so it's resting on the bed, then pull up the other end with his feet and slide it all the way on?" she suggested.

Noah nodded, still too winded to speak.

"Sooner started, sooner finished," she muttered as the two of them hefted the end of the litter. Her muscles were absolutely on fire and she was shaking like a leaf in a fall wind. "I'll hold him here, you get the other end."

She didn't want to push Noah too far, but he had to lift Jack's feet alone. She wasn't strong enough. With a mighty heave, he got the litter's end on the mattress. Slowly they slid it a bit farther.

"Brace him in the middle, Noah."

Noah immediately put his knee under the remaining portion of the litter and stretched his arms out to clamp on tight.

"Ready."

She quickly untied the ropes, then pulled the blanket that was wrapped around Jack until he was more on the bed than the litter. Her muscles were no longer screaming. They were already dead from the strain.

"Pull out the litter now."

Noah carefully inched out the litter. They both breathed a sigh of relief.

"Can you help me pull him a little farther onto the bed?"

Nodding, he came around and they both tugged until Jack was in the center of the bed. Wiping her forehead with her sleeve, she smiled grimly at her partner.

"We did it."

He braced his hands on his knees and hung his head for a moment, breathing like a well-run racehorse.

"Are you all right?" she asked.

"Yes, ma'am. Just rightly winded. Jack is bigger than he looks."

She eyed Jack lying prone and still. She didn't know what Noah was talking about. Jack had always looked big to her.

"Is there anything else?"

She bit her lip and pushed away the despair trying to creep back into her heart. "Pray. Pray as hard as you can."

Noah nodded solemnly. "Been doing that since I heard the rifle shots, ma'am. Do ya want me to fix a bath for ya in the kitchen?"

She glanced at him in surprise. He was as dirty and sweaty as she, but he offered to do more work to see to her comfort. Noah was going to be a fine man one day.

Rebecca smiled. "You are the best assistant a doctor could wish for. Thank you, Noah."

She hugged him quickly. The blush unfurled across his face like a red flag.

"I'll ah...go get that water heated."

He practically ran from the room, and from the sound of it, nearly stumbled down the stairs.

Rebecca turned to Jack, noting his cheeks were looking reddish, too. It could have been the blanket. It was wool. But she knew, with a dread that sank its claws into her heart, that it wasn't because of the blanket. Laying her hand on his brow, feeling the heat, she closed her eyes.

"Oh, Jack."

Taking the pitcher and basin from the dresser, she went back downstairs to get broth to nourish him and some of the melted snow to bathe him. Sure as the sun would rise tomorrow, a fever was going to set in and try to snatch the life she'd tried so desperately to save.

* * * *

Noah spelled her in about half an hour. He had her bath ready, and he'd changed clothes and washed up himself. She thanked him again and went to her bath. She certainly needed it. She smelled of blood, sweat and fear. The past three hours were the worst time in her life, and that fact in itself spoke volumes. Her despair was drifting around her like smoke from a fire, curling its evil wisps through her body, draining her hope.

She undressed mechanically, dropping the filthy dress on the floor along with her underclothes. Thoughtful Noah had left soap, a rag, a towel and a change of clothes for her. She corrected herself. Noah was already a fine man. As fine as Jack was. *Is.* As fine as Jack is.

As she sank into the hot water, she tried not to cry. Truly she did, but it was a losing battle. She gave in and let the tears run their course. She cried for Jack, a wonderful man who struggled for his life, for Nicky, his loving sister and her friend who would be devastated if anything happened to Jack. And she cried for herself. She normally didn't allow herself any self-pity, but in this case, it came part and parcel with the tears. She realized she, too, would be devastated if anything happened to Jack. She liked him, cared for him deeply. Was it love?

She hoped it wasn't. Focusing her gaze on the scars on her wrists, she reminded herself that it couldn't be love. It could never be love or marriage for damaged goods like Rebecca Connor. She was damaged on the inside and out, and bore scars she could never inflict on a husband.

She didn't wipe her tears. They continued to flow freely down her face to mingle with the bathwater.

"Please God," she whispered. "Please don't let Jack die. He has so much, so much to give to Your world. Don't take him yet."

Her chest hurt so much, she could hardly get a breath in. She covered her mouth with her hand as a cry of grief tried to escape. She bit her finger hard. The pain pulled her back from the abyss she teetered on.

Be strong. *Be strong.*

Grabbing the soap and washrag, she began to clean the blood off her hands and arms and from under her fingernails. She scrubbed until her hands were raw. Then she scrubbed her face, cleansing away the evidence of her weakness.

Taking a deep breath, she washed her hair until it squeaked. Rebecca didn't know when another bath would be available, so she took advantage of this one. After she stepped from the tub, she toweled off quickly in the cool air. She carefully removed the wooden angel from the pocket of her filthy dress, then dressed in the clean gown. With a deep breath to fortify her, Rebecca forced herself to wash out her bloodstained dress as best she could. After hanging it to dry by the stove, she put a pot of water on for coffee. It was going to be a long night and she wanted to be prepared. Prepared to do battle against the fevered demons that were closing in on Jack.

CHAPTER EIGHT

As she had predicted, the fever sank its claws into Jack within a few hours. Deeply. And it was a high one. Perhaps high enough to fry eggs on his forehead. Noah hauled in buckets of snow to melt. Rebecca dipped rags into the melted snow and bathed Jack's burning body from head to toe. Then she did it again and again. She had been wrong. It wasn't a long night at all. It was three excruciating days that blended together like hell in a butter churn. But she never left his side. She kept her little wooden angel in her pocket and rubbed it for strength as the hours ticked by.

He was beautiful even covered in sweat, stitches and bandages. Jack was perfect. She tried not to look at his male member; in fact, she couldn't remember ever wanting to look at one, but it would get hard when she bathed him near it. It was impossible to ignore. She had thought any man's penis would be repugnant to her, but inexplicably, Jack's was interesting. More than interesting actually, but she mentally chastised herself over that. Still, though, she couldn't help but notice it. It was, as a matter of circumstance, staring her in the face. Literally. Once she wiped it with the cool cloth and it felt as hard as a piece of wood, then it jerked like it had been poked.

She was so surprised she yelped, jumped backwards and landed on her behind. Luckily, Noah was out in the barn taking care of the animals. She was sure her face was beet red. And parts of her tingled in pain or excitement, she wasn't sure which.

The blood had clotted well on the wounds, and the stitches were holding. They were pink, not red, and there was no sign of infection. However, the fever continued unabated.

Then the delirium set in. And it was so wholly unexpected, so shocking, Rebecca thought she must be caught in a nightmare.

She had dozed off. One moment, she was taking a few minutes to rest her eyes; the next, her arm felt like it was in a bear trap.

"You fucking son of a bitch!" Jack snarled. "You killed him. You killed my baby brother."

He gripped her arm so tightly she thought it would break. His eyes were wild and glassy. The bandage had slipped off his face, giving his wound a sinister look.

"Jack, let go, you're hurting me." She tried to pry his fingers loose, but he was too strong to budge.

He grabbed her other wrist in a punishing grip.

"Hurting you? Hurting *you*? I'll see you in hell, Hoffman." Spittle flew from his fevered lips. "You put me there when I was six years old and I've been saving a warm spot for you."

Rebecca's heart was pounding, her arms were in serious pain, and she was terrified. This wasn't Jack. This was a man in the throes of a nightmare.

"Jack, please, let go of my arms," she said, trying not to whine and sound pitiful, but it hurt so badly.

"You can plead all you like. It won't change shit," he growled.

Noah came running into the room from downstairs, sleep-tousled and bleary-eyed.

"Help me, Noah. He's out of his mind with the fever."

Noah jumped to her side and tried to peel Jack's hands away as best he could. Jack's fingers were like steel bands. The pain in her wrists increased until she couldn't stop her moan of agony. Surely the bones would snap any second.

"Jack, it's Rebecca, not," she choked on the name, "not Hoffman."

Jack seemed not to hear her. His muscles were locked. Noah wasn't making any headway in loosening Jack's grip. It was useless; he was too strong. Becky did the only thing she could think of. She climbed on top of Jack and laid herself flat. Making him feel that she was a woman, not an evil demon from his nightmares. She kissed his cheek and put her lips by his ear. Tears of pain streamed down her face.

"Jack, it's Reb—I mean Becky. It's Becky. Please hear me."

The pressure on her wrists eased a fraction.

"Becky?"

"Yes, it's me. Can you feel me?" She rubbed her breasts lightly against his chest.

The punishing grip eased completely. He let go and wrapped his arms around her instead.

"Hell yes, I can feel you," he said, wiggling his lower half, his *hard* lower half, against her. She could certainly feel that. And he was naked. Oh, my.

"And you feel...delicious." He licked her ear and started kissing her neck.

Shivers ran all the way down her body to her toes. She had to stop this now. He was out of his head and could rip his stitches open. Inspiration struck.

"Noah's coming. You need to let go, Jack. Don't let him see us."

"Shit. Dang kid still has bad timing." When his arms loosened, Becky slid from his grasp to the floor. As she struggled to her feet, her wrists throbbed in pain while the rest of her throbbed in arousal. How could she even *think* of being intimate with him now?

Jack's eyes drifted closed. She breathed a sigh of relief and turned to Noah, knowing she probably looked like a blowsy, flushed saloon girl.

"Thank you, Noah. He's going back to sleep now. Why don't you do the same?"

After Noah left, she wrapped two ice-cold rags around her wrists and sat down to think. What in the world just happened? What did Jack mean he'd been in hell since he was six years old? And how had that monster—she refused to speak his name again—been responsible for it?

* * * *

Jack's fever burned so high, she was surprised blisters hadn't formed on his face. And his delirium continued. Sometimes he talked to his horse; sometimes he spoke to his brothers—usually Raymond—or Nicky, other times he laughed. She felt like she was reading his personal journal, looking into his innermost thoughts. It was disconcerting and it just seemed plain wrong. Fortunately, the anger, the absolute fury, of the first incident didn't happen again. As if all his anger had spent itself in one intense storm.

She was bathing his face with a cool cloth on the evening of the third day—at least she thought it was the third day. Time had no meaning anymore. She was worried. More than worried. She was frightened. Fevers as high and as long as Jack's could be deadly. So she kept bathing him with melted snow. And then things got very, very strange.

She was changing his bandages, beginning with the right shoulder, when he started to cry. She was so surprised, her mouth dropped open.

"Please. Please let me go," he whispered. His voice was small, pleading, very much like a little boy's. He curled into a fetal position, looking like he was trying to make himself disappear.

"I won't tell, I p-promise. Just please let me g-go. That hurts. It hurts a whole lot."

Rebecca's mouth went completely dry.

"It's dark in here and it smells like dirt and potatoes."

Oh, sweet Jesus. He's in the root cellar. She was frozen in place, unable to turn away from him, from his very private pain. Her pulse pounded in her ears like a big drum.

Jack began to sob, big, gulping childlike sobs. "Let me g-go, Owen. Ow! That hurts. Please stop. Please."

It was more than a nightmare. It was hell, just as Jack said. She couldn't swallow or even blink. He wasn't dreaming, he was *remembering*.

"Please stop. Puh-puh-leeeeese." His voice was broken, shattered in pain.

Becky climbed onto the bed and put Jack's head on her lap. Stroking his wet brow, she crooned to him. This was something she was familiar with. Her own bad dreams were just as real. He curled into her and cried, shivering.

"Shhhh, it's okay, Jack. I've got you. I won't let him hurt you again. Shhhhh."

Long into the night, she just held him.

* * * *

Jack smelled lavender. He sniffed. Yup, definitely lavender. Becky smelled like that. He tried to move one arm and felt lancing pain.

What the hell?

Groaning, he opened his eyes and saw small pink roses on his pillow. No, not a pillow. A lap. His head was on Becky's lap. His dick pounced on that fact and hardened like a fence post. He also realized he was naked. Naked on a bed, with his head on Becky's lap. Unfortunately, he felt as if he'd been trampled by a horse. But the soldier was still rising.

The first time he tried to speak, he couldn't even squeak. Licking his parched lips, he tried again.

"Becky?"

She jerked a little, then extricated herself from the bed, replacing her lap with a pillow.

Damn.

"Jack?" She placed a small hand on his brow. "Oh, thank God."

Then she promptly burst into tears. He forced his eyes to focus on her. He was completely bewildered. Becky looked terrible. Her eyes were bloodshot, with huge dark bags under them. Her hair was half-braided and half-flying about her shoulders; her dress was stained, and was that blood? She had bandages wrapped around her wrists; he could see the purple of bruises at the edges. She was blubbering uncontrollably. And he was half-aroused, hell, make that completely aroused, by her, anyway.

"What's going on?" His voice was hoarse.

She wiped her face with a rag and seemed to mentally shake herself. She poured him a glass of water from the pitcher on the dresser and held his neck while he drank what seemed like the sweetest water he'd ever tasted.

"I'm sorry, Jack. It's just that your fever has finally broken. It's been almost four days and I was so worried." Her eyes were still a bit watery, but she was smiling at him. "Thank God it broke."

"But what happened?"

She placed the glass back on the dresser.

"There were two cougars. Don't you remember? You shot the first one. And then..." She paused and licked her lips. Parts of his anatomy twitched. "You c-comforted me and the second one attacked you. He injured you quite badly before I was able to shoot him."

That put a damper on his rampaging lust.

"What do you mean, you shot him?" He tried to shout, but only croaked instead.

She stood and looked like a ruffled bird with her spine poker straight and her blowsy hair. "You were being mauled by the beast, Mr. Malloy. I had no choice."

"You sure as hell did. You should have run like a bat out of hell and gotten Noah."

Jesus, the thought of her facing down a male cougar gave him gray hairs.

"I beg your pardon?" she said through clenched teeth, tapping her fingers on the dresser with a glare. "If I had waited a moment longer, there wouldn't have been enough of you left to stuff in a sausage casing."

With a huff, she started to walk out of the room.

"Wait. Where did you get the bruises on your wrists?"

She glanced down at her wrists in surprise. "I'm fine. They don't hurt at all."

That was certainly no answer.

"I will be back with Noah, fresh water, and linens. And perhaps you may remember your manners enough to say thank you. And please don't curse."

With a swish of her wrinkled dress and a whiff of lavender, she left the room.

Well, hell.

* * * *

Within a minute or two, Noah brought the water and with it came Becky and an armload of fresh sheets and towels.

"These are the last of the sheets, so we need to wash the ones you're using." She set the sheets on the chair. "Let's get you cleaned up first."

She was all business, but so gentle. She removed the soiled bandages, then washed him in warm water and soap, mindful of all his wounds. He was, to say the least, surprised by how many stitches were in his body. They were so even and small, he knew his little seamstress had done them. He even complimented her on them.

She blushed. She actually *blushed*. "I did what I could."

Noah helped her wash his hair. Now that did feel wonderful. Her sharp fingernails raking his scalp clean. He shivered from the pleasure of it.

"Are you cold? We'll hurry it up."

"Mmmmm. No, I'm not cold. That wasn't a cold shiver, darlin'."

He peeked out from under one lid and saw her gaze shift lower and couldn't help the grin. She knew *exactly* what kind of shiver he was talking about.

After rinsing the soap out of his hair, she patted him dry with a clean towel. Frowning, she gently bathed his cheek. It felt tight and raw.

"What happened to my face?"

"A scratch. A rather deep one, I'm afraid."

He tried to lift his hand to touch it, but her hand stopped him.

"You'll rip your other stitches out if you persist in thrashing about."

He certainly was not thrashing, for Pete's sake. He just wanted to touch it. Feeling like a petulant child, he twisted his hand and grabbed her wrist instead. She winced and sucked in a sharp breath.

"Now are you going to tell me what happened to your wrists?"

She shook her head.

"Then I'll have to see for myself."

Ignoring her refusal and her pitiful attempts to stop him, he unwound the bandage from her wrist. When he saw deep bruises, formerly purple, now turning a nice shade of bluish yellow, bruises that were in the shape of big fingers, his stomach dropped to his feet. He'd hurt her. Dammit to hell, he'd hurt her. No one else in this house had fingers that size.

"Becky, I..."

She pulled her wrist away and retied the bandage quickly. "It's okay. I told you they don't really hurt anymore."

"That's a goddamn lie."

Her head snapped up and her lips tightened. "I've asked you before, and I've told you before, don't curse."

"The hell I won't."

"The hell you will." She clapped her hand over her mouth, looking mortified.

He grinned slowly, the tight, painful cheek protesting the entire time. "Don't curse, Becky."

Her pink cheeks turned even pinker. "I can't believe I just said that."

He took her hands in his and gently pulled them to his lips, kissing the bandages that covered the bruises he'd inflicted on her.

"I can't tell you how sorry I am. I would never, ever hurt you."

She seemed like she was about to cry, dammit.

"I know, Jack. It's okay."

He shook his head. "No, it's not. I hurt you. I really hurt you."

She pulled one hand free and cupped his wounded cheek. "No, that wasn't you. It was a nightmare that was controlling you. The real Jack wouldn't hurt me."

He closed his eyes in the face of her forgiveness. Noah cleared his throat.

He had forgotten the boy was even there.

General Becky took command in a blink. "Noah, help me roll him so we can change the sheets."

Fresh cool sheets surrounded him in minutes. The smell was infinitely better.

"I want you to drink some more water and try to get some broth in you. We tried, but it wasn't easy while you were fevered."

He curled his lip. Broth. Baby food. She narrowed her gaze at his expression. She poured another glass of water from the pitcher on the dresser. Her small, surprisingly strong hand supported his neck as he drank. His whole body was shaking from the effort to perform such a simple task.

"Until you get some *broth* in you, you're going to be weak," she stated, an eyebrow quirking up. "Your stomach hasn't had food in days. We don't want another mess to clean up if you eat solid food too quickly."

A polite way of saying you'll get sick on my shoes, so take it slow.

"Okay," he said grudgingly, feeling—and sounding—like a child. "Broth, but I refuse to like it."

She laughed a bit. He tried to smile, but his eyelids suddenly felt like they weighed twenty pounds apiece.

"Sleep, Jack. Just sleep now."

She pulled the blanket up and tucked him in, then kissed his brow. No one had done that for almost twenty years. His last view before he fell asleep was her liquid gray eyes looking at him with concern and something else he knew he wasn't ready to explore.

Something a person who did the dance of the damned should never accept.

CHAPTER NINE

Rebecca shut the door behind her with hardly a sound. Walking to Nicky's bedroom, she sat on the bed and covered her face with shaking hands. She was spent, emotionally and physically.

Dropping to her knees on the floor, she clasped her hands, bent her head, and thanked God over and over for sparing Jack. A man she was sure she was falling in love with. It was exhilarating and frightening to find herself in love, while knowing she could never have a life with him.

Mechanically, she rose, undressed and crawled under the quilt covering the bed, still gripping her wooden angel. There were no sheets, as they'd been sacrificed for bandages, but she didn't care. It was a bed and she hadn't really had rest in days.

It was time to sleep.

* * * *

She woke to the low murmur of men's voices. Groggily, she sat up and realized she had slept the whole afternoon away. The quilt slipped off her shoulders as she stretched her aching arms over her head. It was no use, she still felt like death warmed over. It was almost sundown and shadows were dancing on the walls. She was thankful at least that the sun was shining—that meant it wasn't snowing.

She climbed out of bed, slipped her dress on, then crept quietly into the hallway. Padding along in her stocking feet, she bypassed the guest room without notice and went downstairs. In the kitchen, she found a clean dress, chemise, soap, a towel and washcloth, along with her brush and hairpins on the table. Noah continued to surprise her with his thoughtfulness. He knew her things were still in the guest room where Jack was recuperating. There was even warm water in the reservoir on the stove. She put some in a bucket; then undressed and washed up quickly. After donning her clean dress, she worked the brush through the tangled snarls that used to be her hair. She braided and pinned it after five minutes of silently berating herself for being to lazy to take care of it properly.

Crossing to the stove, she decided to put together supper. The broth she'd made was gone from the pot. Noah must have fed Jack already. She told herself she wasn't disappointed. She was glad he'd eaten, even if it had been Noah who had fed him.

She put a batch of biscuits in the oven, then fried up some bacon and brewed coffee. A tin of canned peaches completed the meal. When the biscuits were done, she made up a plate for Noah and another plate to bring upstairs.

"It sure smells mighty good in here, Miss Becky."

Noah stood in the doorway, smiling.

"I've made some supper, not the kind to sing praises for, but enough to fill your stomach." She gestured for him to sit. "You need to eat and then get some rest yourself."

Noah sat. "Yes'm, but I still need to check on the animals before I go to bed."

"Is Ophelia still melancholy?" She poured two mugs of coffee. At his confused expression, she asked instead, "Is she still sad?"

"Yes'm, a bit, I think. But it's better than yesterday."

Each day could be better. For a horse, the pain of losing a baby faded more quickly. For a horse. She left Noah happily inhaling his food and carried a plate mounded with food and the mugs of coffee upstairs.

* * * *

She heard Jack sigh dramatically right before she crested the stairs.

"I smell bacon. And biscuits. And I get broth. Baby food. I'm going to gnaw on my arm if I don't get some real food soon."

Rebecca stifled a grin and put on her most stern face. When she stepped into the room, every thought of scolding Jack immediately flew out of her head. He was propped up against the pillows, shirtless of course. The tone of his skin, a faded bronze telling of his outdoor proclivity for going shirtless, contrasted sharply with the white of the sheets and bandages. His wavy brown hair was mussed as if he'd run his hands through it. One large lock had fallen on his forehead. His bright blue eyes regarded her with what she could only determine was joy, and he was smiling. He absolutely took her breath away.

Her heart was pounding. The blood was racing around her body like a crazed tornado. She was mortified to feel the prick of tears. This man, this man who had probably had his fair share of ladies giggling over him, was happy to see her. Her. Rebecca Connor. The scarred, used spinster who spent her days talking to a sewing machine. She tried desperately to swallow the lump in her throat. Jack, bless his heart, rescued her with his usual sense of humor.

"Am I going to have to arm wrestle you for that chow? Or are you going to share?"

She found her smile again and was able to walk over to him.

"Of course I'm going to share. But I don't think you're ready to feed yourself."

He scowled. "Can I at least make a pitiful attempt?"

She set the coffee mugs on the dresser and sat on the chair next to the bed. Eyeing his bandaged shoulders, she was hesitant to say yes. He had no idea how deep the cat's bites had gone.

"Please?"

Well, that did it. She couldn't refuse him. Not after he asked so nicely and politely.

"All right, but let me take a look at your wounds first," she said as she set the plates down by the coffee mugs.

"As long as I get a slurp of the coffee. I'm about to cry for wanting it."

Grinning at his foolishness, she brought a cup to his lips. Tilting it slightly, she let him blow on the steaming brew. A jolt of pure lightning went right down her arm as she watched his lips purse as if to kiss the mug. Lord above, the man could kiss like an angel. She had to maintain rigid control of her arm or risk burning him because her hand shook. He took a few noisy slurps then fluttered his eyes and smacked his lips.

"Ah, heaven."

It was amazing how easily Jack could make her smile. Setting the cup back down, she sat on the side of the bed and leaned over to untie the bandage on his left shoulder. It was the deepest wound. Unwrapping the bandage, she was pleased to see the wound was still pink. She glanced at his face and felt like a rabbit in a snare. His pupils were dilated and his lips slightly parted. His nostrils flared.

Desire.

"God, you smell good." His voice had deepened. It was huskier.

It was up to her this time. He made no move to touch her, but he might as well have. Her nipples tightened and rubbed against her chemise. She was damp between her legs and felt as if the room was suddenly two hundred degrees. His gaze fell to her breasts and he licked his lips. If possible, her nipples grew even tighter. He looked back up to her eyes.

"Kiss me."

His low command wasn't necessary. She apparently had already decided to kiss him. She licked her lips and saw the pulse in his strong throat jump.

Desire.

"Kiss me, angel."

She nodded then lowered her lips to his. Fluttering her eyelids shut, she kissed him. His lips were hot against hers, so hot. Like tiny licks of fire sparked from the contact. Unskilled at what to do next, she let her instincts take over and ran her tongue over the seam of his lips. He shuddered and his mouth opened to fuse with hers. Their lips seemed to be as one. Tongue met tongue in a slow, sensual dance. She leaned closer, desperate to rub her breasts against him. They were painfully tight. She could feel his heart beating a frantic tattoo within his chest. One kiss turned into two, then three; then she lost count. She was lost in a haze of sensuality she never thought to experience.

When his right hand cupped her breast, she almost cried with relief. His thumb flicked the engorged nipple while he caressed the rest. She moaned with pleasure so keen, she was lightheaded from it.

Releasing his mouth, she sucked in a big breath and opened her eyes. Gazing into Jack's eyes, she saw her own hunger reflected. That's when she realized the hardness pressed against her hip was him. His own arousal. She couldn't stop her reaction. A flash of panic danced down her spine, but she quickly suppressed it. This was Jack. He'd never hurt her. He must have seen something in her eyes because his hand dropped from her breast and he looked embarrassed.

"Don't even think of apologizing, Jack." She gave him a quick hard kiss, then sat up and forced herself to continue checking his wounds.

She was thankful he didn't apologize. It was her problem, not his. Of course, he had been present when she'd revealed all of the painful details of it in the sheriff's office last year. Her cheeks burned with that realization. He knew a lot, but didn't know all of it. Thank God for that.

For a moment, she thought maybe he was trying to seduce her because he knew she wasn't a virgin. Perhaps he assumed she gave her favors away on a regular basis. Ashamed of her wayward thoughts, she chastised herself for them. Jack wasn't capable of it, nor did he need to prey on dried-up, non-virgin spinsters. No doubt women threw themselves at his feet. A sour thought.

"Lemons?"

She blinked. "Excuse me?"

"The look on your face. Looked like you'd been sucking on a lemon."

"No, nothing like that. Just feeling, well, old."

His eyebrows shot up toward his hairline. "Old? Becky you've got to be about my age. And I'm certainly not old."

"Well, I mean old in experience."

This time he couldn't help but look surprised. "Experience? Honey, unless I'm completely off the mark, you are not old and you are as naïve as they come."

She smiled. "I'll take that as a compliment, however backhanded it was. Not sorry, are you?"

He knew she wasn't talking about their conversation. "No, I'm not sorry."

Staring into his beautiful eyes, she saw passion and warmth. No disgust, no remorse, and thank God, no pity.

"Can I have some food now?"

She laughed, enjoying the moment of peace with this wonderful man.

* * * *

It was the best meal he ever had. They ate and talked and laughed. Becky was smart, witty, and able to take a tease, too, unlike Nicky, who blew up like an overfed fire. Jack was entranced by Becky. He was kicking himself for avoiding her for the past six months. He'd missed out on what it was like to know Rebecca Connor.

"And then," she gave a ladylike snort, "the pickle we found ourselves in was a whole lot more than we expected."

"So tell me why you decided to dress the neighbor's very large dog in its owner's Sunday best dress and, pardon me, knickers?"

Her eyes were full of mirth. "She was a sour old puss. Forever scolding us for things we didn't do. Belinda and I got our share of discipline for things we hadn't done. We thought it was time to do something daring."

"And you came up with this brilliant idea and never expected this dog, who you said was as big as a pony, to chase you two up a tree?" He was trying to picture her scrambling up a tree, a little version of Becky with flyaway blonde curls and smudged petticoats.

"Well, no, we really didn't expect it. The dog had been quite friendly to us previously."

Jack laughed. "Well I'd have a mind to chase you up a tree if you put me in a dress, too."

She smiled back at him. "That would be something to see."

"So what happened next?"

She bit her lip and fiddled with the half-eaten biscuit in her hand. If he had been feeling more hungry, he'd have snatched it from her and eaten it before she could react. "We were stuck up the tree for three hours. That mean old woman left us up there for spite. Even letting the dog rip up her dress while he barked and danced around under the boughs of the tree."

"Did your parents punish you?"

She shrugged a slender shoulder. "I think they wanted to let our time up the tree stand as our punishment. But with old Mrs. Jenkins breathing down their necks, they gave us two weeks of double chores and no desserts for a month."

He humphed. Some punishment. "I guess your parents didn't ever whoop you?"

She shook her head. "No, they didn't." She suddenly looked so sad, so desolate, that Jack's heart flip-flopped.

"Becky, I'm sor—"

She stood quickly. "Let me clear these dishes so you can get some rest."

As she fussed with gathering the remains of the meal, Jack studied her face. Yep, there were untold secrets behind those bottomless eyes. Did he dare push that door open?

"What happened?"

He wasn't asking about the dog and she knew it.

"They died. In San Francisco."

San Francisco. Where she and her cousin had been kidnapped and the nightmare of their white slavery ordeal had begun. Suddenly he didn't want to hear any more; he opened his mouth to stop her but it was too late. She pushed the door open wider.

"My parents were older than most. They never expected to have a child at forty-two, but they did. Me. And then when Belinda was orphaned at five, they adopted her. When we went on holiday, I was twenty-one, Belinda nineteen. My parents were sixty-three. The trip from Michigan was hard on them physically, but they insisted on coming. Nothing would change their minds. Their girls were not going unchaperoned. Funny, isn't it? We were walking together, but Bel and I had a brisker pace and were a block ahead when it happened."

He felt light-headed and nauseated. There were spots in front of his eyes.

Stop.

"My father had a heart attack running after the carriage we were thrust into. He died two days later. My mother passed on within three weeks."

He made a choking sound right before his supper came barreling back up his throat. Becky had good reflexes; she had the water bucket under him before the worst hit. Then she held his head and wiped his brow.

God, why? Why did you have to punish these innocent people?

"Poor, Jack. I'm sorry. The food was too much, too soon."

He was shaking and so soul-deep sick he felt the prick of tears. It wasn't the food that made him sick. It was the guilt. Two more people were dead because of him. How many lives had he destroyed because of his cowardice?

"I'm sorry," he choked out.

She shook her head as she wiped his face with a cool cloth. "You don't need to be sorry. It's not your fault."

He pushed away her hands. She jerked back like he'd slapped her.

"Yes it is, dammit. All of it. I could have stopped him before you were taken, before your parents died, before Logan was killed, dear God, before that poor boy died by his own hand, before Nicky lost three years of her life running. Don't you understand? I ruined your life."

She was silent. Jack turned his face away from her, too cowardly to face her accusing eyes. He could see their shadows on the wall. Hers was as still as a tree. He didn't want to explain any further. Jesus, it felt like great gobs of coals were burning him. Like he was already roasting in the hell of his own making.

"When you had a fever, you talked in your delirium. Aside from the obvious cursing, you spoke of being hurt, begging someone to stop, that you wouldn't tell anyone."

His mouth was frozen. He couldn't speak, couldn't even breathe.

Shut up. Shut up.

"It sounded like you were reliving a memory of when you were a child." She paused and rested her small hand on his shoulder. He shuddered. "Jack, were you the first person Owen took into that root cellar?"

Oh, God, oh, God. Make her stop.

"Jack, it's not your fault. None of these things that happened were your fault."

Jack felt it coming on. And there was nothing—absolutely not one frigging thing—he could do about it. Tears burst from him in great sobs, his throat was clogged and years of pain rushed forth in a wail of anguish. He tried to hide it, turning on his side while his injured shoulder screamed in pain. Soft, cool hands stopped him. She climbed on the bed and wrapped her arms around him, stroking his back and head as he cried like a babe.

"You don't have to say anything. Just let it out. Let all that poison out."

He clung to her like a lifeline in a sea of pain. Her sweet lavender scent surrounded him in an invisible shroud of love.

"I'm sorry," he kept repeating as she rocked him through the night.

* * * *

Jack finally fell asleep. Rebecca dared not move from the bed yet. She wanted him to sleep. As she wiped her own tears away, she studied his face. He blamed himself. He had been taken advantage of by a monster as a child and he blamed himself. Human beings were the only perverse creatures on earth skilled at self-flagellation. How could he possibly feel guilty?

Rebecca gently traced the contour of his cheek where the wound was healing. She felt as if she were standing on a precipice, looking down instead of up. It was time to stop looking down, to just take that leap and learn to fly.

She was in love with Jack. His was a kindred spirit, a wounded warrior. Together perhaps they could heal each other. There were a great many ifs to that, and she knew she was opening herself up to potential devastation. But in looking back over the course of events, it was almost as if fate had brought them together. That they were meant to be together. Their lives had been touched by the same people, for good or evil. And when they touched each other, the absolute rightness of it nearly made her cry. She knew she could search the world and never find another man as connected to her as Jack. She loved him.

Jack might not feel the same way about her, and if he did, those feelings could change when he found out what she had done. His darkest demon had been brought to light already, and she accepted it and him, without question. Only Belinda and a doctor in Nebraska were acquainted with her darkest demon. Telling Jack would rank right at the top of her "I can't do this" list, but if she hoped to have a future with him, it must be done. She could only pray her confession wouldn't drive him away.

CHAPTER TEN

The next morning, Jack cracked his eyes open and found Becky sitting in the chair next to the bed reading a book with a steaming mug of coffee in her hand. She was wearing the dress with the little pink roses on it. He knew every time he saw roses again he would always think of Becky's lap.

In a flash, he remembered everything that happened. Instead of gut-wrenching pain and guilt, he only felt sadness. Perhaps telling her was what he needed. Damned if he'd tell Nicky she was right. Now, of course, he felt a surge of nervousness around Becky. Would she blame him? Think him less of a man? Or would she, God forbid, never forgive him?

She looked up and saw his eyes open. Too late to play possum now. Instead of anger, censure, or recrimination, she smiled. In her beautiful eyes, he saw acceptance, concern and something more. Something like...love. Was he ready for that? And why did his heart pick up?

"Good morning. Would you like some coffee?"

He nodded. She stood and placed her book and mug on the chair. She started toward the door, but apparently changed her mind and walked back to the bed. Perching on the side, she leaned over and took his face in her hands.

"You, Jack Malloy, are a wonderful courageous person. I am proud to know you."

How could she possibly say that to him of all people?

She smiled and kissed his forehead. "I hope you can forgive yourself one day, Jack. Although I don't think there is anything for anyone to forgive. I don't blame you, and I certainly don't hate you. Far from it."

Then she kissed his lips softly. As she exited the room, she turned back to look at him and, by God, winked.

Jack promptly fell the rest of the way in love.

* * * *

She came back with a biscuit and coffee for him. She instructed him—that was the only thing he could call it—to eat very slowly. Since he was as weak as a kitten, it wasn't like he could do much but go slowly.

"Would you like me to read to you?"

He did. So she read a Jane Austen novel to him. It was actually very good, although he wouldn't have selected it to read on his own. Becky had a natural talent for reading aloud. The words floated around her like butterflies on flowers. Without quite meaning to, he went back to sleep with her soft voice echoing in his ears.

* * * *

And so it continued for two weeks. They were the two best weeks he could ever remember. He slept each night, without nightmares, only erotic dreams of Becky. She slept on a pallet on the floor beside the bed.

She sat with him, read to him, cooked for him, and best of all, played chess with him. She was very, very good. He was too. Growing up, he'd been an avid participant in the Malloy family chess tournaments. He'd never won—Ray would hands down beat anyone—but he was usually in the finals. Playing with Becky was a challenge, and sometimes he won and sometimes she won. They were equally matched, apparently. In more ways than one, he decided.

With Noah's help, he got up and tried to stand, and the next day to walk. He'd never felt so helpless in his life. But Becky praised him more than anyone ever had, and over the most minute things. Like standing on his own two clumsy feet.

Becky was an incredible woman. He never laughed so much as he did in her company. Women were definitely not his specialty, and his experience was limited to a sister, a mother, and a sister-in-law. Slim pickings. But somehow, with Becky, it didn't feel like a chore, as if he would choke on the next word that popped out of his mouth. She made him feel relaxed, and he could be the real Jack, not the silly, goofy clown with a quick temper everyone expected him to be. If he didn't enjoy something, he told her. If he did enjoy something, he told her that, too. She accepted all of it without question, as a friend would. In truth, in the weeks they'd been together, she had become the best friend he'd ever had. Closer than Logan or Nicky had ever been. The thought wasn't frightening; rather, it gave him a warm feeling in his chest.

He loved her.

* * * *

Coward. That's exactly what she was. A dyed-in-the-wool coward. Punching the bread dough as hard as she could, Rebecca continued to chastise herself. How many times had she had the opportunity to tell him, but had held back, unwilling to take the final step to trusting him. The past two weeks had been heaven on earth, the best time of her life, bar none. Rebecca didn't want it to end, nor did she want to see Jack's horror when he found out what she had done. It was something she could barely face herself. She was surprised there wasn't a bright yellow streak running up her back.

Noah interrupted her self-flagellation. She was glad of the distraction.

"Miss Becky?"

"Yes, Noah?"

"We're getting real low on supplies. The snow has melted quite a bit, enough so I can get a horse through it and into town." He was shuffling his feet and looking beyond her. She noticed he acted a little jittery around her now. What was that about?

"You're right. This is the last of the flour," she said, gesturing to the dough in front of her. "Do you want me to make a list?"

Noah's cheeks turned pink. "Yes'm. Miss Nicky is teaching me my letters, and I read purty good. My writing ain't so good yet."

"I'd be happy to. Give me two minutes."

She finished kneading the dough, then laid a cloth over it to rise. After rinsing off her hands, she got a paper and pencil from Nicky's writing desk in the living room. Rebecca sat at the kitchen table with Noah after she examined the larder. He watched her avidly as the pencil moved over the paper. He definitely had a thirst for knowledge that Rebecca was happy to water.

"Do you have your empty saddlebags?"

He nodded. "Yes'm, and a blanket with some jerky, hardtack, and water."

She smiled at him. "You are a smart young fellow, Noah. What a fine man you'll be."

He stammered and blushed and looked so uncomfortable. She helped him bundle up warmly and shooed him out the door.

"Get your horse ready. I want to check with Jack to see if he needs anything."

Still smiling, she went upstairs to talk to Jack. When she walked into the room, she gasped. That stubborn jackass was standing without help again. Standing next to the bed, holding onto the back of the chair.

"John Gideon Malloy. You get back in that bed this instant."

He gripped the back of the chair tightly, like it was a sturdy branch on a tree.

"It's been two weeks, Becky. I need to get back on my feet without Noah under me like a human crutch. I've been lying on my back for so long, my feet forgot how to work."

She pursed her lips, determined not to fall for his charm. "Well, you can try it again later. For now, I must insist that you get back into that bed."

Waggling his eyebrows, he said, "Only if you join me."

The thought was more than tempting, but she couldn't possibly let him know that. Instead, she huffed in impatience, and crossed the room briskly, determined to give him a set down. Then she wrapped her arm around his naked waist. Lord above, he was only wearing a sheet. The first touch of skin to skin was like lightning. It made her sizzle everywhere. Especially, embarrassingly, between her thighs. She tried to concentrate on guiding him back to the bed, but it was so hard. *He* was so hard. The feel of muscle, sinew, and bone beneath her hands was erotic. His scent was richer than anything store-bought. It was like breathing in his essence. It traveled straight to her heart and set the rest of her on fire.

Jack lost his footing as he lowered himself back onto the bed. His weight pulled her down, too. Right on top of his hard, naked self.

This time she gasped from the pleasure. She never knew just touching someone, albeit an entire someone, could be so stimulating. And he was so warm, like a furnace. Her breasts were pushed against his chest so tightly, she knew for certain he felt the hardening of their tips. She felt the hardening of his body quite clearly.

She stared down into his eyes, the pupils wide with desire. Desire for her, Rebecca Lynn Connor. Something she thought would never happen. He shifted beneath her and his engorged shaft pushed against her, in a spot that sent a bolt of pure heaven through her from top to bottom. His indrawn breath spoke of his own mounting desire. He deliberately moved again and she hissed.

Again.

The thrumming in her lower body was part pleasure, part pain. She wanted more. She wanted him to push against her again. She wanted him to push *in* her.

More.

She couldn't help it. She moaned. He buried his nose in her neck and started nibbling.

"Becky, hell, that's... Damn, that's so good."

She tried to catch her breath. "Please don't curse."

She felt him smile against her overheated neck. "That's one of the things I lo—"

"Miss Becky?" Noah called up the stairs.

"Shit."

What was he about to say? *Love?* Was he about to say *love?*

Becky scrambled off him as quickly as she could, her body protesting every inch that was separated from that hard, naked man.

"Yes, Noah?" Her voice was husky.

"Was there anything Jack wanted?"

Blue eyes met gray with a heat so intense she was sure it burned every inch of her. He quirked up one eyebrow.

"From town," she blurted. "Noah is going in for supplies."

"It'll take him all day to get there with the snow drifts so high," he commented.

"He's prepared and we are getting very low on supplies."

Why, she was babbling.

"Ask him to get me a bottle of whiskey down at Abe's place. You used half of Tyler's supply on me, and it never went down my throat." He smiled and her knees wobbled.

She nodded her head like a puppet and fled the room without even chastising him about ordering liquor. Perhaps she needed a glass of it herself.

* * * *

Jack was so hard, he thought he might have to take care of himself to ease the pressure. Didn't want his body to explode from lack of blood to the brain. When she had fallen on him and they'd rubbed together so nicely, he thought he'd embarrass himself by coming before he touched anything but sheet. Noah's interruption saved him, but ended a moment of exquisite sensuality. That Becky could be so passionate, so responsive, amazed him. Just another reason to love her. She was perfect.

Then it dawned on him. They were going to be alone. Completely and utterly alone. He grinned at the empty room.

CHAPTER ELEVEN

Rebecca sent Noah on his way, and then ran into the kitchen to splash cool water on her face. This situation with Jack was out of control, way beyond the boundaries of her normal, if boring, existence. She loved him, wanted him, ached for him, but did she dare? What did she have to lose? She wasn't a virgin after all. She could lose his respect, his friendship, perhaps even Nicky's friendship. That was supposition, of course. She could lose nothing, but gain back a part of her she'd lost four years ago in a root cellar in Wyoming. Love, passion, pleasure all for the taking, but did she dare reach for such a prize?

She needed a bit of normalcy. They were friends. Something she had wanted to solidify before they became lovers. Lovers. Just the word made her temperature go up a few degrees. She had no doubt Jack would be a good lover, even great, just as she had no doubt they would become lovers. And to be able to see him and touch him naked. Just the thought... The room was suddenly too small. And she was thinking too much.

And thinking wasn't helping at all, so she dried her face and hands and got to work cleaning up the kitchen. After that she would find something else to do in the kitchen until her indecision stopped plaguing her. Putting fresh wood in the stove, she stirred the embers and watched the fire come to life. Yes, the fire was definitely coming to life.

* * * *

Jack was wrestling with his indecision. Should he tell her? Should he confess the rest of it? She deserved to know, especially if this afternoon was going to be "it" for them. He shouldn't be calling making love "it" but he was as nervous as a newborn calf. The truth of it was, he was scared. Yep, no hiding behind it like a schoolgirl, he was scared shitless. He hadn't been scared when facing that scrap of humanity he'd finally killed last year. He refused to believe Tyler's bullet had reached that bastard's heart first. He'd been furious, and that left no room to be scared.

But now, ah, faced with the very real possibility of getting naked with the woman he had hopelessly fallen in love with, his fear knew no bounds. Should he tell her? No one, not even one of his brothers and most especially Nicky, knew that he'd never lain with a woman before. That he turned into a pile of jam and couldn't even think about getting naked with a woman, that he had run. And kept running for years. Loving Becky had put a bridle on that particular racehorse. He didn't think he could run from her, run from the thought of making love to her. He had only seen a naked, completely naked, woman once when Ray had taken him to the whorehouse for his "initiation" at the age of sixteen. Ray didn't know, because Jack had paid off Ruby, that the initiation had been an hour of playing cards.

Imagining Becky naked had taken up a lot of his time when he'd been lying in the damn bed recuperating. He'd had more than his share of tent poles rising under that sheet. He spent many nights with a painful bedtime companion that he had to see to or risk never sleeping. If he decided to make love with Becky, he ruefully wondered if he'd miss his hand.

It wasn't that he *couldn't* make love with her, but he was afraid he *wouldn't.* Life had become so mind-numbingly familiar that this experience with Becky had slapped him out of that complacency. He didn't know if he was ready, but that didn't seem to matter. He was riding the storm, helpless to do anything but hang on.

He hadn't experienced anything but fear and self-revulsion around women until now. Until Becky. He ran a damp palm over his face and realized he had at least four days' worth of grizzle on his cheeks. Oh, hell. He couldn't smile and charm his way out of that. He'd scrape the skin right off her. How romantic. He frantically looked around but no shaving razor and soap magically appeared. Noah had shaved him the last time, but apparently had cleaned everything up and took it with him. He had to find a razor. Slowly, he pushed himself off the bed and went on a hunt.

* * * *

Becky was brushing her hair. Like she was preparing for something. Like she was preparing herself for *him*. The thought rippled through him like a skittering leaf, leaving goose bumps in its wake. He couldn't remember the last time he'd had goose bumps. And he couldn't really see her clearly since he was spying on her through a crack in the doorjamb. Skulking like a little boy. Nevertheless, he watched. He could not, it seemed, stop himself.

Her hair crackled when she pulled the brush through it. It glittered like sunlight on a pond. He'd dreamed of touching her hair, of removing her hairpins and shaking the long strands out, of feeling her hair caress his bare chest and his equally bare cock. Lord above, he had a damn hard-on again. From thinking about her hair, for pity's sake. Who knew what would happen if he thought about her beautiful breasts...touching them, licking them, biting them...

He must have made some kind of noise, because she turned toward the door, her eyes wide.

"Jack?"

Think about something else. Like little kids pulling taffy. Like Grandpa Joe without teeth.

Okay, better. Less rampant. Less...stiff.

"Jack?" she repeated.

"Yes, I'm here," he managed to reply, voice cracking like a teenage boy's.

"Did you need something?"

His knees weakened at the question. God, he needed so much. So damn much. He needed *her.*

"Jack, what's wrong? You know you aren't supposed to be walking around without one of us."

He cleared his throat. "Nothing's wrong...um... I wanted to shave."

"Oh."

"My things are still under my bunk in the barn. So I thought I'd see if Tyler left anything I can use." As useless excuses went for spying on someone, that one took the cake.

She opened the door and he got his first real look at her glorious sunlight-colored hair. He leaned against the doorframe so he wouldn't fall. She had stolen his breath away.

"Your hair."

"My hair?" She reached out and touched the top of her head. He wanted to bury his hands in the strands and hang on.

"It's incredible."

Her eyes regarded him steadily but her hands fidgeted with her brush. She was as nervous as he was. Finally she dropped the brush next to her.

She wrapped her hand around her hair, twisted it and pulled it up on the back of her head. "I was going to put it up—"

"No, please don't. Please...leave it down."

She nodded and released the golden waterfall down her back. "Okay."

They stared at each other for what seemed like an hour before he realized how silent it was.

"Um, about that razor?"

She jumped a bit at his voice. "Tyler may have left one. You're welcome to look." She stepped aside to allow him in the room. He could almost see the sexual tension between them.

"You know you shouldn't be walking around unassisted," she said again.

He grinned. "I plan on doing a lot more than walking. I've got to build my strength again."

She blushed. His hands itched to touch that rosy cheek and see if it was as soft as it looked. Like a pale pink rose. Pink rosebuds. Becky's lap. Oh, hell, the damn tent pole. Clenching his wayward thoughts and his fists, he walked into the room. After some foraging, he found a razor in the washstand, but no soap. He was looking on the dresser when the sound of water pouring into a basin had him turning his head. Becky hadn't put her hair up. Instead she brought him warm water for his shave. She laid a clean towel and soap beside the basin.

"Thanks, Becky."

He tested the razor with his thumb, then closed it and set it down. It seemed sharp enough. Praying that he didn't slice his throat under her gaze, he picked up the soap, wet it, and began to lather up.

* * * *

She'd never seen a man shave before. Her father had been quite strict in what was acceptable and watching Jack shave was definitely not, especially considering he wasn't wearing a shirt. She watched the muscles in Jack's back tighten and move as he prepared to shave. All that tanned skin was almost too much to look at. It even made her fingertips tingle.

"May I watch?"

He stopped dead. She saw him swallow and close his eyes. "Sure, I guess, if you want to." Opening his eyes, he wiped his hands on the towel.

"I do."

She saw a ripple skitter across those muscles. Like he had shivered, but it wasn't cold in the room at all. In fact, it was hot.

"Okay then."

He opened the razor again and started shaving. The rasp of the razor was loud in the quiet room. Watching him seemed so much more intimate than bathing his fever-ridden body. Well, not to say that *that* wasn't intimate, but *this*. This made her fantasize that this was their house, their bedroom, and Jack was her husband. And for a moment, she saw stars of happiness, but it was only a moment. The pain of knowing it could only be a fantasy crushed the stars to dust. Jack had such a bright life ahead of him. He couldn't be weighted down by a shadowy spinster. Her darkness would extinguish his light, his spark. She couldn't even contemplate a future. Their time would only be now. She wanted to grasp this moment and safely tuck it away in her memory. So that later she could close her eyes and picture him as he was, shirtless, shoeless...hers.

"How are your wounds feeling?"

He flexed his arms a bit. "Sore, a little itchy, but no pain."

"When you're finished shaving, I want to check them."

"Yes, ma'am, General Becky." She knew if he hadn't been shaving, he would have saluted her.

Out of the corner of her eyes, she saw movement. Turning her head to the window, an icicle of fear trickled through her. It was snowing, really snowing, heavily, horizontally. She couldn't even see the barn.

"Jack."

He was wiping the last of the soap off his face. "Almost done."

"It's snowing."

"So it is."

"Noah is out there, on his way to town. Sweet Jesus, that boy is out there in this."

She stared wide-eyed out the window. A woman, a wounded man, alone with limited food supplies and a fifteen-year-old boy, alone in a snowstorm.

"What time did he leave?"

She blinked and shifted her gaze to Jack's serious face.

"About three hours ago."

Pursing his lips, he looked out the window. "Wind is pushing this from the Northwest. He went east, right?"

She nodded.

"He should be ahead of it then. He'll get his supplies and hole up in the hotel in town. He's no fool, Becky. Life has taught that boy a few lessons."

"Do you think he'll be okay?"

He smiled. "Without a doubt. That kid is a survivor. He'll head back when the weather is clear."

"Last time it snowed for three days."

Holy Mother. As she said the words, the full impact hit her. They were alone, completely, utterly alone together. His gaze met hers and a spark of heat flew from him. It was nearly time.

* * * *

Rebecca cleaned up the shaving water while Jack went back to the guest room. Even though he had reassured her, he was worried about Noah. Damn spring storms were very unpredictable. He sent a small prayer that Noah was already in town and enjoying a hot meal at the hotel.

He sat on the edge of the bed and waited. Anticipation began to thrum though his veins like a steam engine. When she finally came bustling in with clean water and bandages, he about jumped off the bed.

"I'm sorry. I didn't mean to startle you."

He shook his head and didn't respond.

"I thought you might want to wash the rest of you after I remove the bandages. It's been a few days, so..." Damn, she blushed again.

He grinned. "Only if you help. I'm still a little sore and weak."

Becky looked at him a bit skeptically. "Let's get those bandages off." She gently untied, then removed the bandages. After examining each wound thoroughly, she touched the stitches on his cheek. "They look marvelous. I can't believe how well you look in just over two weeks. I can take the stitches out of a lot of these."

"I'm a fast healer, and I had the world's best doctor."

She shook her head as she got a tiny pair of scissors and snipped the stitches on his cheek, then gently removed the thread without a lick of pain. She moved on to his right shoulder. "Foolish man. A woman is not likely to be a doctor."

"But you could. You are a wonderful healer."

She didn't shift her gaze from her snipping. "I watched and learned. My father was a physician."

"You see," he crowed. "You could be a doctor, too."

She didn't answer and he could see a bit of darkness hinting around those gray eyes. Something he didn't want this afternoon. No darkness, only light. He decided not to push her any further. She was one of the smartest people he had ever met, and it would be a shame if she thought she couldn't be a doctor because she was a woman. He'd heard of a few, why not Becky?

All but one of his wounds was free of the stitches within ten minutes. "I'm going to leave this one for another week or so. This one was the deepest." She frowned at his left shoulder. "That's where he was biting you."

She looked so serious, so upset. "Becky, it's okay. I'm all right. That cat only scratched me up a bit."

She met his eyes. "I know you're nearly well now, but...I can't explain it, Jack. It was so...so hard for me to see you injured like that."

So she cared for him. His heart did a little dance. Becky could possibly even love him. A burst of joy made him feel about ten feet tall.

She shook her head as if to throw off her maudlin thoughts. "Let's get you washed up."

She rolled up her sleeves, then dipped a clean cloth into the warm water. Her small hands lathered soap on the cloth, then turned, and began to wash him. Her touch was like angel's wings, soft and heavenly. He closed his eyes as she washed his chest and back, humming softly. She gentled her touch around his new scars. Warm water trickled down his skin. It was as close to perfect as he'd ever been.

When she started washing his arms, he opened his eyes and saw her scarred wrist. It was inches from his eyes. Twisted, ropy-looking scars with a purplish undertone. It was the first time he'd ever been allowed this close to them. She froze when she saw where he was gazing and tried to pull her arm away. Jack grabbed both her wrists and brought them to his lips. Reverently, he kissed every inch of the scars, and then pressed them to his chest. The cloth in her hand steadily dripped on his leg.

Her hot tears hit his hands. "They're so ugly, Jack. So ugly."

"No, Becky, they're not."

She dropped to her knees in front of him, unable to pull her wrists out of his grasp.

"Please..."

"Please what?"

The cloth fell to the floor as she put her head onto his knee.

"I won't let you or anybody else tell me these scars are ugly. They show the world how brave, how strong, how alive you are."

"No, I'm not brave," she protested softly. "Not strong. I'm weak."

"I won't hear another word," he replied. He pulled her head up from his lap and forced her to meet his gaze.

"But—"

He placed a finger across her lips.

"You are about the most beautiful thing I have ever had the privilege of seeing, Rebecca," he said, caressing her cheek with his free hand. "You are incredible, inside and out. And I want nothing more than to make love to you."

Tears flowed freely down her cheeks now.

"Jack, I need to tell you—"

"I know. You're going to tell me you've never made love before." She looked surprised. "I have a confession to make...neither have I. I've never lain with a woman, Becky. I think I was waiting for you."

Now she looked completely astonished.

"You mean you've never…"

He shook his head and smiled. "I was waiting for the right woman. For you."

She reached up a shaking hand and traced the new scar on his cheek.

"Then let's learn together." Leaning forward, she brushed her lips across his, once, twice. He wanted to grab her and plunge his tongue into her mouth, but this had to be slow. It had to be perfect.

"Jack," she breathed.

"Yes, angel?" He kissed her cheeks, her brow, then her lips.

"Can we put out the light? And…and close the curtains?"

He saw apprehension in her eyes, but no real fear, and he desperately wanted to ease it. Rising, he pulled her to her feet, and then blew out the lantern as she closed the curtains. The room was draped in afternoon shadows.

CHAPTER TWELVE

She was scared. Terrified that he'd turn from her in disgust. All she had was this time with him to savor. She didn't want her scarred body to ruin it. Her wrists were only the beginning of them.

He started to unbutton her dress and she shivered.

"Cold?"

"No, never that."

She could see a flash of his teeth in the gloom.

"I seem to be overheated whenever I'm around you," she blurted. Now that sounded ladylike.

He nuzzled her neck, the skin on his face smooth from his shave. He smelled like her soap, and like Jack. A heady essence that once inhaled traveled straight to her nipples and into the crux of her thighs. Where she pulsed and ached, a place she thought long dead and dry. But it wasn't dry now, in fact, sweet heaven, it was wet. *Wet.*

He kissed the side of her neck, then nibbled his way up to her ear. His tongue laved it with a gentle rasp that made her hardened nipples into peaks of rock. They too pulsed and ached, hungry for something, anything.

Without her realizing it, Jack had undone all the buttons on her dress and slipped it off to land silently at her feet. He sucked in a breath as he felt her bare skin. She was embarrassed now for him to find that she wasn't wearing anything under the dress. It had seemed like a good idea at the time, but now she felt like a shameless hussy. His big hands cupped her breasts, sending a shudder through her and her thoughts to the wind. Time stopped.

"Becky?" His voice was so husky she barely recognized it. She was trying to get her tongue to work when he, misinterpreting her silence, started to move back. She grabbed his hands a mere hair's breadth from her molten skin and pulled them to her aching breasts.

"More," she murmured.

His breath gusted past her ear, and she felt a shudder pass through him.

"God, woman."

When his fingers tugged at her nipples, she almost melted like hot candle wax. She was still holding his wrists and she could feel what his fingers were doing to her nipples. It was incredibly arousing, almost as if she were caressing herself. If possible, she grew wetter.

His lips reached her own and they were scorching. He groaned down deep in his chest, a groan which vibrated through her. He slid his arms around her buttocks and lifted her up against him. She opened her legs and wrapped them around his waist. Shamelessly slamming the part of her that was wet, pulsing heat, into him. Into his arousal, a hard ridge of blatant desire that should have frightened her. But it didn't. It inflamed her. She moved up and down ever so slightly, the friction and heat making her nearly scream for more. Her bare breasts rubbed against his hard chest. It was the most erotic thing she'd ever felt.

His tongue danced with hers as she wished the part of him she was currently grinding herself against would dance with her other mouth. The greedy wet one that was driving her to clutch Jack's shoulders and hair, and to moan. She was moaning, over and over, not caring how loud or how long.

He lifted his mouth from hers and sucked in a ragged breath.

"Are you sure?" he ground out.

She climbed off him, savoring one last slide against his straining member. Reaching the floor, she stepped back and began unbuttoning his pants. The heat radiated off him like a roaring fire. His breathing was choppy and uneven.

When she popped the last button, she belatedly realized he wasn't wearing anything under the jeans and the hardest part of him now rested in her hands. She should have run screaming from the room, or let go of it at least. Instead, she stroked him. His member jumped in her hands.

"Jeeeesus," he croaked.

He was soft and hard at the same time. With one hand caressing him, she used the other to push his pants down past his hips. She needed to feel all of him. She cupped his balls as he had cupped her breasts. They were tight, warm and amazingly hairy. She loved the feel of him, loved the fact that he was shaking because of her, of desire for her.

"Shit, Becky, you're going to make me come," he whispered against her hair.

"Come?"

He tried to laugh, but it sounded more like a choked sob. "Come, explode, blow, little death, whatever you want to call it."

She continued to run her hand up and down his shaft and her other hand played with his balls.

"Is that how the seed comes out?"

He sucked in a breath. "I forget how straight talking you are."

"Is it? Is that why they call it coming?"

His breath hitched. "Yessss."

She smiled into his shoulder. "You are beautiful, Jack. What do you call it?"

He pulled her hands away from him. She itched to put them back.

"Okay, we need to slow down."

Taking a few rattling deep breaths, he kept her hands back. She tried to move, but he held her firm. "Give me a minute, darlin'. I wanted this to be slow."

"What do you call it?" she repeated. She had to know, because she couldn't keep calling it "it".

He was silent, still breathing raggedly.

"Please?"

He sighed. "I call it my cock."

The word flew like a flaming arrow to land between her legs. Cock. That was exactly right, deliciously right.

"Cock," she repeated. She heard said instrument slap against his stomach.

Oh my.

"Like a rooster, right? May I touch it again?"

He groaned. "Later."

A little disappointed, she opted instead to make him touch her.

"Very well then, later."

He released her hands and she stood there naked in the dusky room with a mostly naked man. And she was unafraid. More than unafraid, she was excited.

Stepping closer to him, she found his hands clenched into fists. She pried them open and laid one on her left breast, and gulping, one between her legs. She thought he stopped breathing.

"I know what to call yours." She felt it jerk again, this time against her arm. "What do you call these?"

He made a strangling sound, but his hands, oh, his blessed hands began to move. His callused finger dipped into her wetness and stroked her from her rear end up to the top of her mound. There he found a nubbin of pleasure that made her want to weep with ecstasy when he began to rub her there.

"What...do...you...call...them?" she gasped out as his other hand kneaded and caressed her nipple.

He hesitated a moment longer; then spoke. "I call this," he grasped her mound, "your pussy." The said pussy pulsed against his hand. "I call this," he pinched her rock hard nipple until she gasped, "a tit."

The words were more than titillating. They were shocking and very, very arousing. She never thought words would excite her. But they did. They roused her along with his magical hands.

"Can we take your cock, my pussy and tits and go to the bed?"

He moaned from somewhere near his toes. "Jesus, Becky, you're going to unman me."

She grinned. "Never. There's way too much man here to ever go away."

* * * *

Jack was so hard he didn't think there was a drop of blood left anywhere else in his body. Her combination of naiveté and downright bawdiness shocked him and excited him to dangerous proportions. He couldn't remember being this hard around a naked woman, and this wasn't just any woman. It was Becky, the woman, the lady who owned his heart. And apparently, also his cock.

"Are you sure?"

Was he mad or simply stupid? He'd already asked her that. Her response was to give him a hand job so sweet he almost came in her hands. Here was a naked woman he was crazy in love with offering, no wanting, to jump into bed with him. And he was questioning it.

She walked to the bed, and through the shadows he studied her. She was a goddess. When she climbed into bed, she was in deeper shadows.

"I've never been more sure of anything in my life. I think we're both tired of being afraid. Come to me, Jack."

He nearly fell on his head in his haste to get to the bed because he forgot his pants were bunched around his knees. Yanking them off, he finally got to the bed and joined her.

The first time their bodies met skin to skin was enough to stop his heart. Every small hair on his body stood at attention along with his cock. It was...it was so right. He belonged in her arms and she in his. How could he have denied it for so long? He ran his hands up and down her warm, soft body. He felt the scars on her wrists, and more on her breasts and thighs. They both had many scars inside and out. Hers didn't detract even a smidge from her beauty.

"I'm sorry," she whispered.

"For what?" he said as he kissed his way down her chest.

"I'm sorry I'm not perfect. And I'm truly sorry you're not the first."

He stopped and moved back up to hold her face in his hands, peering at her beautiful shaded eyes in the gloom.

"Becky, Becky, Becky," he murmured, caressing her pouty lower lip with his thumb. "You are perfect in my eyes. And I *am* the first. The first to make love to you...the first to love you."

Well, hell, he hadn't meant to let *that* slip. Her breath hitched and then let out on a long sigh.

"Jack." She sounded so breathy. "I love you."

He was lost. Utterly, completely lost. Talking was done, over. It was time to speak with their bodies.

* * * *

Jack seemed like a man driven. He licked, nibbled and sucked her nipples until she writhed with need. She tried to grab his cock, but he kept it away from her reach. His hands caressed her everywhere, most especially between her legs. Every pulsing pull on her nipples had an answering beat in her pussy. The sensations were intense, incredible. His callused fingers stroked and rubbed her nubbin of pleasure until she thought she'd go mad.

"Please, Jack, please." She didn't know what she begged for but she needed it. Now.

Spreading her legs, he hovered above her. She felt him nudge the opening of her warmth.

"Yes," she hissed. That was what she needed.

As he slowly sank into her, stretching her, filling her, it felt like time stood still. As if the birds stopped flying, the wind stopped blowing, and the stars stopped twinkling. It was heaven and earth and everything, *everything* at once. When he settled in her fully, when she could feel him hard and deep inside her, she finally breathed. She finally lived.

"God, you are so tight, Becky," he whispered. "So good."

"So good," she repeated.

Then he began to move in and out. The friction and heat were building like a storm. Faster and faster, harder and harder. *More. Again.* She couldn't form a coherent thought.

"Jack."

"Close, Becky, so close."

She knew what he meant now. He was close to coming, to spilling his seed. Now. More. Just a few more strokes. The pleasure that crashed over her was so intense, she was sure she was going to die. Her muscles clenched over and over. Jack shouted her name as he rammed into her so deeply he touched her womb, her heart. Again and again he pulsed against her. And she felt tight, so tight, clenching around his hardness. He collapsed on top of her, gulping for breath.

Her heart was beating as fast as a rabbit's. She felt an answering mad thumping from Jack. His chest hairs tickled her nipples.

"Jack?"

He grunted and then rolled over next to her, pulling her up against him spoon style. Grabbing the quilt from the bottom of the bed, he covered both of them, and wrapped his arm around her waist. He kissed her shoulder and ear, and promptly fell asleep.

"I love you, Jack."

Rebecca snuggled closer, still tingling from head to toe. She closed her eyes and sent a silent prayer up to God, thanking Him. She had truly found what she'd been searching for. Love.

* * * *

He woke with his arms wrapped around her. More at peace, hell, happier than he'd ever felt in his life. She loved him. *She* loved *him.* He knew he must have a stupid smile on his face as wide as the Big Horn Mountains, but he didn't care. She loved him.

Her scent filled his lungs along with a musky scent from their loving. Just one good whiff and he was hard as a fence post. His hands seemed to be taking their cues from his pecker because they started wandering up and down her soft, warm skin. God, she felt so damn good. He traced the curve of her waist to the swell of her hip. She shifted on the bed. He continued his meanderings up to her beautiful breasts, the nipples were surprisingly hard already. She was awake, or at least her body was.

Making his way from her shoulder across to her neck, he alternated kissing, licking, and nibbling. Feasting on her tender flesh like a starving man. When he started pinching lightly on her nipples, she shuddered.

"Jack," she murmured.

"Good evening, darling. Care to go for a ride?"

"A ride?"

"Mmm...a ride on me, your noble steed."

She played along with his silliness as his hands continued to play with her nipples. He wished he could see what color they were.

"Will I need a riding outfit?"

He smiled into her hair. "No. What you're wearing is just the thing."

His hand stroked its way down her stomach to land in the nest of curls. Dipping a finger into her honey pot, he found her wet already. Jesus, his cock grew another inch. He pressed it into the cleft of her buttocks and gritted his teeth. So damn good.

"Looks like your saddle is ready, too."

She moaned and opened her legs wider.

"Let's ride, cowboy."

The night's loving was slower, more sensual, but no less intense than the mad passion of the afternoon. As he slid into her, she was just as tight, hot, and wet.

"Jack," she breathed.

The sound of his name on that breathy whisper was almost enough to make him come on the spot. His balls were tight with need.

"Touch me."

Her command was his wish. He stroked and petted her, played with her nipples. He kept up his pounding rhythm into her core. Delicious, incredible Becky.

"Jack, I think I'm going to come."

Her words tightened his balls even more, his shaft tingling with pleasure. He was about to come, too. He rubbed her clit harder, she moaned louder; then began to buck wildly as her release took over.

"Jack!" she screamed.

Her clenching felt like a velvet glove driving him over the edge. He pumped into her as deeply as he could. All the way. All the way home.

The rush of sensation stole his breath. He never knew, never dreamed it could or would be this incredible. He almost blacked out from the pleasure of it.

"Heaven," she whispered.

Yes, that was it. It was heaven.

* * * *

They were lying in each other's arms, quietly caressing and absorbing the feeling of just touching.

"There's something I need to tell you." Jack took a deep breath. "You were in my dreams, my nightmares for a long time. I don't know why, but you were. Your...experiences and mine were all mixed up in my head. And I was so afraid to see you again, to face what it was I was running from."

She put her hand on his cheek. "I'm sorry."

He grimaced. "There's nothing for you to be sorry about. It was my twisted logic. I'm ashamed of how I avoided you the first week you were here. You didn't ask to be in my dreams, and...well, you're going to think I'm crazy."

"I wouldn't."

He believed her. "There was this bond between us, like my pa has with the men he fought the war with. I don't know how to say this...like two people who had been in a battle, seen the worst that human beings can do to each other..."

"Like kindred spirits."

"I guess that's as good a word as any. I just felt connected to you."

She nodded against his chest. "I felt it too. Like there was something between us."

"Like a river, or the tide that ebbed. And it gave me a feeling of..."

"Peace," she said.

"Yes. That's it exactly. And I wasn't sleeping very well."

"I could tell. Your symptoms were classic sleep deprivation."

He was surprised. "Really? You knew?"

"Mmm hmm. I knew the first time I saw you in the kitchen. When you protected your sister from my nefarious plot," she teased.

He was embarrassed by that whole thing, but knew she was only teasing. "You are pretty strong when you want to be, Becky. You could probably take her down."

She laughed. "Not likely. Tyler would squash me like an ant."

"Good point."

She was silent for a moment, her fingers twirling in the hair on his chest. "You started sleeping after they left, during the blizzard, didn't you?"

"How did you know?"

She shrugged. "Same way I knew you hadn't been sleeping. The human body is easy to read. What was it?"

"What was what?"

"What was it that helped you start sleeping again?"

"You." His answer was as simple as it could be. It was Becky. It was being near her, touching her, talking to her, hell, just breathing the same air. "I can't explain it any better than that."

"You don't have to, Jack. You're my anchor, too."

He leaned back and looked into her eyes. Had he ever in his life felt so close to anyone? Close enough he could read her thoughts and she could read his? This is what he wanted, needed, craved. He hugged her close and silently thanked God for making this angel who she was. His.

* * * *

The next time she woke, it was morning. There was sunlight to greet the day, which told her the snow had stopped. Thank God. She'd had enough snow to last her a while. It also meant the room was relatively bright, even with the curtains closed.

Rebecca tried to will away the tears pricking her lids. This, this was so wonderful, this passion they'd shared. Jack had taught her the things she never thought she'd learn. And love. This was definitely love. She loved him so much it would nearly kill her to let him go. But she had to. Jack had healed her. She had healed Jack. The darkness was still there in the recesses of her heart. She could never be completely whole. There were too many pieces to put back together. Jack deserved someone with a whole heart.

He rolled over; then kissed her softly. Grinning widely, he said, "Care for a ride this morning?"

"You're incorrigible, Jack."

"More like insatiable. I'm afraid you've released a beastie."

He growled theatrically and began to lay sloppy, noisy kisses on her neck. She laughed and tried to pull back from his silly kisses. The quilt slipped down. He stopped when his gaze focused on her breasts. His smile faded. Oh God, he'd seen the scars. She tried to cover them with her hands, but there were too many. He pulled her hands away. And dear sweet saints, were those *tears* in his eyes?

He reached out a shaking hand and lightly touched one of the burn scars on her breast.

"Becky. How they hurt you. I...I—"

She placed a finger over his lips. He shook it off and took a shuddering breath.

"That you had to suffer any of this is...is tearing at my heart..."

"Jack, it was a long time ago. It's okay."

"No!" His vehemence startled her. "It's as far from okay as anything could be. They hurt you. Jesus Christ, they burned you, didn't they? Over and over. God, I can't imagine anyone hurting something so beautiful."

As he had done with her wrists, he began kissing each scar. Showering them with his healing love. When he reached her belly, he lightly traced the few stretch marks she had. She begged God not to let him ask about those yet. Not yet. He continued down to her legs until he'd touched every last scar.

"You're beautiful. Skin like milk and honey. Nipples like peaches, ready to be plucked."

The lump in her throat was more like a boulder. How could he think she was beautiful and not hideous was beyond her reckoning. In a minute he'd declare his undying love and do something really stupid like ask her to marry him. In a minute, she might say yes. She had to stop it. Now.

"There's something I need to tell you."

The graveness in her voice made him pull back to his own side of the bed. Better, more breathing room at least. She pulled the quilt back up to cover herself.

"There are only two people who know this story. A doctor in Nebraska and my cousin Belinda. I'm going to tell you because..." her throat closed for a moment and she clenched her fists and willed it to reopen, "...b-because you deserve to know."

He leaned back even further. His blue eyes were intent. He was listening.

"After Belinda and I moved to Nebraska, we found a doctor who tended to our...wounds very discreetly. A nice old man whom we came to trust completely. That was why I went to him when I discovered I was with child."

His indrawn breath was more like a hiss. She stared at the quilt, unable, unwilling to look him in the eyes. God, this was harder than she thought.

"I cannot even begin to describe the depths of despair I was mired in. My parents were dead, I'd been kidnapped, raped and tortured, and then this. A child. From all that evil. I cried for months, willing the baby away, but it didn't work of course. Belinda kept me fed and the baby grew."

She paused a moment to take a shaky breath.

"I thought about how the boy, Jacob, had escaped his pain."

This time he really did hiss.

"But I knew I couldn't do it. I talked to God a lot, and finally, I think He answered me. It was a child, but it was also a blessing, a gift that many people hope and pray for, but never receive. I decided to put the baby up for adoption. When she was finally born, she was a healthy, perfect child. Blue eyes, fuzzy blonde hair, ten fingers and toes. I held her once." She forced herself to swallow. "Gave her a name, then gave her away."

She didn't bother to wipe away the tears. The guilt still ate at her like acid after three years. She gave away her child because she couldn't bear the shame of looking at her and knowing she was conceived in rape. She was ashamed of herself now. Ashamed of how little she could love a child.

"What did you name her?" was the only question he asked.

His soft voice made her teeter on the edge, but she held on. "Hope. I named her Hope."

* * * *

Jack stomped his feet into his boots, then yanked on his jacket, hat and gloves. He practically pulled the door off its hinges to get outside. He needed to do something violent, and because none of his brothers were around to pick a fight, snow shoveling it was.

A baby. Jesus ever-loving Christ.

Confused and shocked, he shoveled his way with a vengeance to the barn. It was only about six inches of snow so it wasn't even a challenge. Then he grabbed a pitchfork and mucked out the stalls when he got to the barn. He definitely needed to roll in some shit. After all she'd been through, she'd been forced to have a child, too. He was so angry, so frustrated, he wanted to howl at the moon and tear his hair out.

And what about what you did, Jack? That could result in a baby too.

His blood ran cold. Holy shit. They hadn't used any kind of protection. And dammit, he knew all of them. His big brothers had passed on all of that knowledge. He hadn't needed it, nor thought of it, until now. And there was no force on earth that could have pulled him out of her when he was coming. So they could have made a baby, either time.

A baby... His anger started to deflate and instead he started to feel something different. Hope.

* * * *

Rebecca listlessly washed and dressed. Making her way to the kitchen, she built up the fire and made coffee and dough for bread. While the dough rose, she stared out the window, seeing nothing. The slate gray sky promised more snow later.

He ran. That was the polite way to put it. She told him the ugly truth and he ran. Not that she blamed him, but when he ran he took her heart with him. Nothing beat in her chest anymore. It was empty.

She wasn't angry, and she certainly didn't blame him. If she was honest with herself, what she felt was relief. She just hoped he would forget her and move on to love someone else. Someone worthy of his love and his children.

CHAPTER THIRTEEN

Malloy ranch, that same morning

Tyler stared hard at Hermano. The son of a bitch hadn't changed an iota in six months. And here he was, back in Tyler's face. That bastard bandito was exclaiming over Nicky's pregnant belly, dressed in his standard brown clothes and chaps with that godawful neckerchief. The pistols strapped to his thighs were no doubt loaded. He must have left his bandolier on the horse, but his knife, ah, that frigging knife, was in a scabbard on his back. And Nicky, damn her hide, was hugging him. It was enough to make Tyler sick.

"What the hell are you doing here, Hermano?" he growled.

Nicky frowned at him and narrowed her eyes.

Hermano's smile vanished. "I hear things. Things about you and *Roja,* so I come to tell you. To warn you. I try to make it to your house, but the snow was blowing too hard. I stop here at *Roja's* papa's house for a rest."

Nicky sat on the sofa and patted the cushion.

"Sit, *amigo.* Tell us."

Tyler clenched his jaw and let the bastard sit next to her. She cut her eyes to him once. The love that twinkled out at him was enough to stay his hands from Hermano's throat.

"You know a man named Gaetano Juarez?"

Nicky and Tyler both shook their heads.

"He also goes by the name Guy."

Nicky blanched. "There was a Guy that worked for...for Hoffman. The foreman. He was a greasy pig. Gave me the shivers every time I saw him."

Hermano nodded. "*Si*, that is him. He escape from prison a few weeks ago, *Roja*. He tell everyone he is going to cut the hearts out of those who put him there."

If possible, she got paler. Tyler started to cross the room, but she shook her head at him. "I'm fine. Go on," she urged Hermano.

"I ride to you as soon as I hear this."

Tyler crossed his arms over his chest. "There's more."

Hermano stared at Tyler. "*Si*, gringo, there is more. Guy found out where your ranch is. He had a two-day lead on me, but I think I cut it to one. I am happy to find you here though."

Nicky made a croaking sound. "Oh my God. Rebecca. Guy was one of them, Tyler. He's one of the men who...who was in the root cellar with Owen." She turned to Hermano. "My friend, my brother, and our boy, Noah are there. All alone."

She burst into tears. Hermano reared back, his eyes wide with shock. If he weren't so worried about Nicky, Tyler would have grinned at the bandito's expression. Instead, he quickly crouched in front of his wife and gathered her into his arms. She needed him more than he needed to laugh at Hermano.

"Jack is capable, magpie. He can handle one mangy outlaw."

"No, gringo. Not one, three."

Tyler's heart quickened. "Three?"

"*Si*, three. Two more *hombres* he found that used to work for the same *bandejo*."

He met Nicky's terror-filled eyes. Damn, Jack didn't stand a chance against three of them. He was just a rancher, regardless of his penchant for Colt pistols.

"We ride. Now."

Hermano nodded and they both rose to leave. He heard Nicky struggling to get off the couch and chase them. He turned and pointed a finger at her.

"You are staying here, woman."

She stuck up her chin at him and scowled. "I know that, Calhoun. I was going to pack some food for you."

He nodded then set out to gather up the rest of the Malloys to ride like hell for the Bounty Ranch. He prayed they would get there in time.

* * * *

Jack returned to the barn with the wheelbarrow after dumping the muck into the heap. He was surprised to see three strange horses in the barn.

"Where the hell did you come from?" he said under his breath.

He dropped the wheelbarrow and went to check the horses. Poorly maintained, low-quality saddles that smelled of unwashed bodies and piss. The horses were driven until they looked like they'd drop. They hadn't been rubbed down or watered. One of them appeared dead already, but just hadn't fallen over.

Where had they come from? And more importantly, where were the three men who had left them here? He had a really, really bad feeling about this. Why would they leave their horses in the barn unless they meant to be in the house for a while...?

Becky.

Oh, sweet Jesus. She was alone in the house. He almost went tearing off screaming her name. His heart was beating so hard he thought it might burst. But he slowed himself down and took a few deep breaths. He needed a plan to get into the house, find and stop three men, and retrieve his woman. And not get himself killed in the process.

The first things he needed were his guns. Luckily, they too were still under his bunk. Then he had to think of a way into the house. There must be some way he could sneak in without anyone knowing it. He knew this house; he'd been here often enough. *Think, man, think.*

He paced back and forth like a whirlwind in front of the pitiful horses, smacking himself over and over in the forehead, willing some spark of smarts to leap up and ignite. If Tyler were here, he'd know exactly what to do. But no, Jack had to stay and work on the addition while Tyler was gone with Nicky...

The addition. Yes, that was it. Jack clapped his gloved hands together, startling the horses. The window was installed and you couldn't see it from anywhere but the back of the house. Tyler had hung a blanket up where the door would be. It looked like the entrance to the pantry, just on the other side of the kitchen. If he was lucky, they hadn't noticed it was a room. A room with a window. That was his way in and perhaps their way out.

She was his woman, his love, his future wife. He had to save her.

* * * *

When the knock came at the door, Rebecca thought it was Jack. Perhaps he was trying to be polite and apologize properly. She hurried to the door, but when she swung it open, it was three strangers bundled up against the snow. A prickle of fear crawled up her neck. She was sorry she hadn't put her hair up in her usual bun. She felt exposed and frightened.

"Can I help you?" she asked, her voice surprisingly steady.

They pushed their way into the house and slammed the door behind them.

"Where are they?" the biggest one asked.

"W-who?"

"Calhoun and that red-haired bitch."

Tyler had been afraid of this. He'd even voiced it aloud to her in Nebraska last year, but she'd made him see past the threat. Now that threat was very, very real and literally staring her in the face.

"I don't know who you're talking about. My husband and I just bought this place a month ago."

The biggest one snorted. "You're a bad liar, *niña*."

That word. That voice. Oh, dear God. She knew that voice. As he unwrapped the scarf from his head and took off his hat, her dread grew. When she finally saw the face, a little older, with another scar or two, the nightmare was real again. It was Guy. A man who had used her body for his own pleasure while he'd burned her breasts with his cigar. A man who liked pain with his pleasure.

Curly black hair, now liberally sprinkled with gray, topped a hard, bristly face with droopy mud-brown eyes, spiky black eyebrows and a crooked nose. His teeth were brown from tobacco stains and his belly hung over his filthy clothes like a pregnant woman's. He smelled so sour, she gagged. But it wasn't just seeing him. It was knowing that he knew who she was. God, that voice. He had called her *niña* then, a voice and a name she'd heard in her nightmares.

She felt woozy. Couldn't get a breath in her lungs. *Don't you dare faint.* She dug her nails into her palms until the pain snapped her back. She was no longer the naïve twenty-one-year-old virgin who had screamed for pity and met agony. She was stronger, tougher, and she would be damned if she'd go down without a fight.

"Get out."

Guy's smile was ominous. The other two snickered. "Why would we do that, *niña*? It's cold out there. And here you are, warm and inside. The wagon and most horses are gone from the barn. So it is you and it is us."

The barn? They didn't see Jack? Did he really leave without saying goodbye? Where was he?

"And you will tell us where they are," he said, still smiling. "I will enjoy taking that information from you."

"Like hell," she snarled. Jack's cursing had obviously rubbed off on her.

Rebecca ran into the kitchen like her feet had wings, or perhaps she was riding on the wave of panic that had taken hold of her. She heard the men's start of surprise, but knew they'd be on her in a flash. Skirting the table, she ran for the rack behind the stove where Nicky kept her sharp knife. It was a risk. If she went after the knife, they would block the doorway to outside, but if she ran outside without a weapon or a coat, she'd be dead anyway. Her heart was thundering against her ribcage and she swore she could actually feel their breath on her neck.

Reaching out as she ran past, she snatched the long-handled knife. Her palms were slippery and the knife nearly fell, but she caught it, though slicing her palm open in the process. Switching the knife to the other hand, she spun around, her hair swinging madly in front of her face, temporarily blinding her. She growled with rage and swiped it back to face her attackers.

Only one, Guy, had followed her into the kitchen. He was grinning that awful, evil smile she'd seen so often in her nightmares. She could hear booted feet upstairs. The other two men must have gone to check for others. She prayed Jack would stay in the barn. He was too weak to fight off three people. He had to live, while she...she could die as long as she knew *he* would live. And she'd take as many of these bastards with her as she could.

"*Niña*, you have a weapon, I see," Guy said as he slowly walked toward her.

"Get out of this house!"

He stopped and perused her from head to foot. She suppressed a shudder of revulsion. "How are you going to stop us, *niña*? You could tell us where the bounty hunter and that red-haired witch are, and we let you go free. Is a good deal, no?" He had moved a few feet closer.

"*Nada*," came a shout from upstairs.

Guy's eyebrows rose in surprise. "So you tell the truth, eh? No one here but you and us." He rubbed one filthy hand over his crotch. "Well, we can wait for them right here. Why don't you cook us up a meal with that little knife? If you don't want to cook, I can think of something else good to do."

"I said, get out of this house before I slice your belly open." She waved the knife in the direction of his paunch.

He leered at her breasts and licked his lips. "I'd love to see those tits again."

That was when Rebecca decided she wasn't just going to threaten to kill this dreg of humanity. She *would* kill him. She raised the knife and ran at him, screaming like a banshee.

* * * *

Jack unsaddled the three strange horses quickly, stripping off the weapons. There was a jumble of clothes on the back of one of the saddles. Women's clothes. In disgust, he wondered who they'd murdered to get them. There was a wool coat among the clothes, just about Becky's size. It stank a bit, but he set it aside. If his plan worked, they'd need a coat to keep her warm. He saddled Sable and Ophelia, not missing the irony of planning an escape on the two horses Tyler and Nicky had traveled on together, when he was the hunter and she the prey. He threw the strangers' gear in an empty stall, and attached their weapons to Sable's saddle. Leaving the five horses near the back door of the barn, he ran upstairs to get his guns from his bunk. After he wrapped the gun belt around his hips, he tied the straps to his thighs in record time. He came back down, quickly stuffing his gloves in his back pocket—he'd need his hands free to draw if needed.

Jack paused at the barn door to peek outside. He could clearly see the path to the house. The packed snow was full of boot prints. They were definitely in the house. He had to physically restrain the urge to run hell bent for leather to the house, to quell the rage and helplessness he felt. Three men were in there with Becky. Alone.

Stop thinking about it. You're no good to her if you're not in control of yourself.

Before stepping outside, he checked to make sure his guns were loaded. Slipping them back into the holsters, he was comforted by their weight. Sending a quick prayer to the Man upstairs, he left the barn.

Keeping low to the ground, he crossed the hundred yards to the house, constantly looking for trouble. It seemed to be more like a hundred miles that took hours to reach, when it was probably less than a minute. He was surprised to find he didn't feel weak from his healing wounds; instead, he knew he could race a mustang across the desert and win. The blood pumping through his veins was as hot as the sun. He was as furious and as scared as he'd ever felt in his life. His breath came in small puffs in the cold air. The biting edge of that cold even hurt his teeth. It must be below zero outside.

When he got to the porch, he flattened himself against the side of the house. He heard someone shout "*Nada*" from inside. The fear for Becky was increased tenfold. That was a man's voice, a strange man's voice. And dammit, he needed to get in there to her. His fists were clenched so tight even his teeth ached.

Crouching low to pass under the living-room window, he hurried to the back of the house. He was as quiet as possible, walking in the powdery snow to avoid crunching ice with his boots. He finally reached the window to the addition. Gently sliding the window open—and thankful that Tyler had oiled it— he paused a moment before continuing. As he was climbing in, he heard Becky's voice.

"I said, get out of this house before I slice your belly open."

Becky's shouted command nearly knocked him on his ass back out the window. He gripped the sill until his fingers ached to avoid falling. She sounded so fierce, so angry, so unlike herself. Like a wolf warning her prey. He was proud of her and terrified for her. He hauled himself through the window and eased in as quietly as he could.

He crossed the room and barely moved the curtain to look into the kitchen. What he saw was beyond what he expected. Instead of helpless, she was furious. A raging goddess. Her hair was hanging down, one hand was bloody, the other held Nicky's sharp cooking knife. A tall, dirty dog of a man stood with one hand hooked on his belt loop, the other rubbing his crotch. He heard him say something about her tits and she went completely berserk. Screaming, she ran at him with the knife raised. Jack knew more than a moment of fear.

Holy Christ.

The man stopped her easily. Twisting her around so she was pressed up against him back to front, he squeezed her wrist until the knife dropped to the floor. And still she fought; she fought like a wildcat. He grabbed hold of her bloody hand and licked the palm, tasting her blood. While she tried to kick him, he turned until Becky was pressed up against the wall and started humping her even as his other hand roamed up and down her body. Rage, pure violent rage poured through Jack's veins.

"More, *niña*, more. Fight me." he thought he heard.

Praying he could be quiet as a cat, he pulled out his gun and snuck closer to them. He had never experienced such anger, such hatred for another human being. Not even for Owen Hoffman.

How dare that piece of shit touch her.

When he crept close enough, he brought the butt of the gun down as hard as he could on the man's head. He crumpled like a house of cards, bringing Becky down with him. As she struggled, still screeching, to get his legs off her, Jack knelt down and touched her shoulder. She screamed again.

"Becky, for Chrissakes!"

She turned to him and burst into tears. Okay, so now she was going to be a sad, crying woman. He pressed his finger to his lips and pulled her out from underneath that pile of horse shit.

"Let's go," he whispered in her ear. "As fast as you can, darlin'. Good thing you're wearing shoes."

Fighting the urge to put a bullet in the outlaw's brain, he half-dragged her back to the addition. He scrambled out the window then held his arms out for her. She dropped down easily.

"Keep to the soft snow."

She nodded that she'd heard his command. Together they ran to the barn as fast as they could. When Becky stumbled, Jack didn't miss a beat. He simply scooped her up and kept running. Behind them, he heard a shout and the front door banging open. Slamming into the barn, he practically threw her up on Ophelia, and then pushed the plank down against the front doors to bar them.

He grabbed the wool coat he'd saved from the outlaw's booty and shoved it at her. "Put this on. I know it stinks, but it's wool."

Visibly shaking, she took the coat, and put it on in a blink. When Becky wanted to be, she was a good little soldier. He put his hand on her thigh.

"We've got to ride now, honey. Are you ready?"

She grabbed the reins and looked at him with wide eyes. "Ready."

Pushing open the back door to the barn, he jumped up on Sable and grabbed the reins of the other three horses.

"Hiya!" he yelled as they took off into the cold.

* * * *

Rebecca heard the shouts of the outlaws behind them as they galloped off across the snow-covered land. Wearing a dress, pantalettes, and not much else besides an odiferous wool coat, she bounced painfully astride Ophelia, the big mare, terrified of falling off. She only knew how to ride sidesaddle. On a street. On a docile horse. Not on a half-wild mare. She dared not tell Jack she had never ridden astride. Their very lives depended on her staying upright on this horse. So she did, with gritted teeth and pounding heart.

She heard gunfire and tried to crouch as low as possible on the saddle without falling off. Not an easy feat when she couldn't even see through the blinding tears from pain and cold. She felt a sharp sting on her right arm—the same arm with the bloody hand that was throbbing in tune with the horse's hooves. Could she possibly be any more miserable? Oh yes, she sure could. The sting, she realized, must have been a bullet grazing her. Because now her arm was burning and blood trickled down her arm.

Dandy. Just downright dandy.

She hung on, mentally picturing their lovemaking from the day before. It was the only image that kept her sane for the next hour as they rode on and on.

And then it started to snow. She tried not to cry. She truly tried, but the pain, the cold, the numbness, and now the snow grew to be too much.

"Jack!" she cried.

He glanced behind her and must have seen something in her face that told him she was on her last leg.

"Whoa, boy. Whoa."

Pulling hard on the reins, he brought the four horses to a stop and dismounted. She mimicked his movements and

Ophelia obediently stopped as well. Or it could be she was lovesick for Sable and didn't want to leave her man.

Rebecca was getting giddy and a little stupid. Loss of blood and shock for sure.

He let the reins of the other three horses go, then slapped their rumps until they took off into the snow. Jack came over and looked up into her eyes.

"Are you okay? I know you're cold, but if you can hang on a bit longer..."

She bit her lip to keep from screaming "no" and instead mentally catalogued her aches. What was the most pressing?

"I need to bandage my hand and my arm. I'm losing blood and getting a little woozy. It should only take five minutes."

His eyebrows slanted down. "What do you mean, your arm?"

"I think a bullet grazed me back there when we were riding off, but I'm not sure."

He cursed colorfully and looked at her with murder in his eyes.

"I need to go back there and kill those bastards."

"No, you don't, Mr. Malloy. Give me your neckerchief, no, better yet, rip it in half and tie it around my wounds and we can go." She was as calm as she could be. "And don't curse."

He cursed again as he pulled off his neckerchief and obediently ripped it in half. "Which arm?"

She held out her right arm and he wrapped her hand first, so gently it brought tears to her eyes. He looked so upset at the sight of her blood. Dear, dear Jack.

"I'll take the coat off this arm so you can put the bandage under it."

She gritted her teeth against the pain of the wool rubbing on the open wound as the jacket slid off. Jack examined her arm carefully, pulling the dress sleeve up so he could get a better look.

"Well?"

He frowned. "It's a graze, not too deep, but I'll bet it hurts like hell."

She frowned at him, knowing he was cursing to keep her mind occupied on something other than the fact she'd been shot.

It was a minute before he tied off the bandage and drew the dress sleeve back down. By then she was shivering uncontrollably. He helped her put the coat back on. Lord above, it surely did stink, but it was warm. Too bad she didn't have one for her nearly bare legs.

"I think there're some caves in a few more miles. Tyler told me about them a few weeks ago. Can you hold on?" His gaze was full of concern.

She nodded. He cupped her neck and kissed her softly.

"You're a helluva woman, Becky Connor."

"Mount up, cowboy. It's time to ride," she said.

* * * *

It was more than a few more miles. It was more like six. Six miles and two hours of excruciating cold, pain, and terror. Rebecca hung on through sheer will. Her body had given up at least forty-five minutes before. The wind that whistled and screamed around them blew her ears and nose full of snow. She breathed through her mouth, in short little spurts. She was sure she still had legs and feet, but they were completely numb. One plus was she couldn't feel the slice in her palm or the bullet graze on her arm.

"There they are. The hills with the caves. I'm sure of it. Tyler said the tree out in front looked a buffalo. That must be it," came Jack's voice through the swirling snow.

She didn't respond, just hung on as Ophelia plodded along behind the gelding. When the horse stopped, she gripped the saddle horn to keep from falling off. Jack appeared beside her.

"Wait here. I'll be right back. I need to scout the caves."

She nodded, but didn't speak. She had to keep her jaw clenched so the chattering teeth didn't take off her tongue by mistake.

Please hurry, Jack.

* * * *

Fortune was with him. The second cave Jack looked in was large enough to shelter them and the horses. He couldn't see much past the opening as it was too dark, but the ceiling was at least twelve feet high. It would do.

He marked the outside of the cave by scratching the letter J in the stone, and then hurried back to Becky and the horses. The incline was too steep for them to ride the horses up, so he would need to lead them. He slid down the last ten feet and ran. Reaching Sable, he took the bedrolls off the saddle and belatedly realized he'd forgotten to put the saddlebags on.

Damn. That meant no food. Water they could deal with by melting snow, but no food was a bigger issue. He also prayed to God he had some matches in his pocket or they wouldn't even be able to light a fire to get warm. He walked over to Ophelia.

Becky was leaned over the horse's neck, hugging the mare. She was either getting body heat or trying to keep from falling off. Jack knew she was done for. He wasn't surprised she'd lasted this long. Becky was an incredibly strong person, if a bit bullheaded. When he'd insisted she take his gloves, she'd refused, but he'd held stubborn. He was glad he had, because without keeping her hands warm, she wouldn't have been able to hang onto the horse at all.

Reaching up, he grasped her by the waist and cradled her like a child. She was as cold as a block of ice. He popped the bedrolls on top of her and turned to climb back up to the cave. He wasn't worried about the horses; Tyler and Nicky had trained them to be ground-tied. They wouldn't wander.

Climbing back up the hill with a full-grown woman in his arms wasn't easy. Twice he almost fell face first, but caught himself just in time. It certainly wouldn't be a good thing to flatten Becky with his one hundred eighty pounds on a snowy, rocky hillside.

When he reached the cave, he was panting and shaking from the effort. Becky was as silent as the snow. That, more than anything, made him forget his tiredness and move quickly. He set her down gently and leaned her up against the wall.

"Hang on, honey."

He dug through his pockets with mounting dismay and realized he didn't have any matches or a flint.

"Son of a bitch."

"Don't curse," came the little, tired voice from the corner.

"Becky." He knelt next to her and peered at her in the gloom. "My rescue wasn't much of a rescue. No food, no water, and no matches. We're really going to have to cuddle, darlin'."

She mumbled something, then tried to pull off his gloves.

He laid his hand over hers. "No, keep them on."

She glared at him. "Let go of my hands, Mr. Malloy. I think I may have some matches in my pocket. If I could get these huge gloves off, I may be able to reach them."

He reluctantly released her hands and stayed silent as he saw her struggle. He didn't stop her, but he'd be damned if he didn't offer to help.

"Can I get them for you?"

She stopped and sighed. "You may as well. I can't feel enough of my body to know my toes from my ears."

"Which side?"

"I don't remember. Probably my right."

He reached under the coat and tried not to be distracted by the feel of her soft body. He fumbled around a bit before she snapped at him.

"You don't need to determine my corset size, Jack."

He grinned. "I'm just trying to find your pocket. Be patient. I don't have dresses so I don't know where the danged pockets are."

He finally found the slit in the side for the pocket. Reaching in, he hoped it wouldn't be empty. It wasn't, but it only held the little wooden angel he had given her. The fact that she carried it in her pocket warmed his heart in the bitter cold.

"No matches in this one. Can we turn you so I check the other side?"

She tried to move herself, but it was like watching a fish flopping on a rock. He picked her up and set her on his lap instead.

"Oh, you're so warm, Jack," she breathed against his chest.

Bound to get warmer if she wiggled any more. Determined to check her other pocket quickly, and without getting distracted by those tempting breasts, he maintained his composure long enough to locate it. This time before he reached in, he said, "Please God." A little prayer couldn't hurt.

At first he thought it was empty, but he reached in a bit further and found two slender pieces of wood. Matches.

"Got 'em. Two of them, Becky."

He leaned down and gave her a big, smacking kiss on her cold lips.

"Now, let me get you bundled up so I can go get those horses out of the snow and find some kindling."

He laid out one bedroll a bit deeper in the cave, then scooped her up and set her down. Tucking the other around her like a swaddling baby, he made sure there was no part of her beside her little face that wasn't covered.

Her big gray eyes looked out at him, full of fear and resignation.

"Are we going to die, Jack?"

Her question nearly knocked him off his feet. He didn't want to say no, and he couldn't say yes, so he ignored the question and kissed her forehead; then ran from the cave.

* * * *

Jack hadn't answered her question, so really, he had. They could die. She knew that. She also knew if she didn't warm up soon, she would die. He didn't know how close she'd been to total collapse before they'd stopped. She was slow, awkward, and disoriented, and very, very sleepy. Signs of exposure to extreme cold. It wasn't such a bad way to die, as far as dying goes. It wasn't painful, once you got past the numbness. But she didn't want Jack to die. That would be infinitely more painful than dying herself.

He came back five minutes later with an armload of snowy wood.

"I found a downed tree just on the other side. It should work just fine. Let me bring the horses in before I start. They can help block the wind."

After he led in Sable and Ophelia, he quickly stripped off the saddles and rubbed them down with their blankets. The horses nickered and pushed their heads at him as he took care of them.

He piled some stones together to make a ring for the fire, then started ripping the smallest of the kindling into shavings to fuel the fire. When he had it set up, he took out a match. As his gaze met hers, she saw fear and desperation there. He was afraid for her, for them, but he wasn't giving up without a fight. Becky hadn't given up, but she was losing hope. She wanted to believe they'd survive.

"Ready?" he asked as he raised the match.

She nodded. He struck the match on one of the stones and it flared to life. The smell of sulfur was strong as he desperately tried to light the shavings. Blocking the wind and the light with his body, he could probably hardly see what he was doing, but he kept at it. After about ten seconds, he cursed and dropped the match.

"Don't even think about telling me not to curse, Becky."

She stayed silent. She knew it wasn't the time to be upbraiding him for his language. Their lives were in danger.

"Try the other one, Jack."

He took out the second match. "You'd better work, you little bastard."

Again he struck the match and held the small flame to the shavings. As he held the match tightly, he muttered, "Come on, come on, light, damn you."

Rebecca prayed like she'd never prayed before.

A puff of smoke curled up from the shavings. She never thought she'd be glad to see smoke. Jack leaned down and blew softly on the little fire, then again and again. Finally, it became bigger. Jack fed a piece of kindling into the flames. It got bigger, and soon it began to really look like a fire. Ever so carefully, he built the fire up until it was a small, popping blaze. The wood was wet, but hopefully it would continue to burn. When his eyes met hers over the flames, there was triumph and a smattering of happiness.

"If you hadn't had those matches, angel, we'd surely be done for."

She found the energy to smile at him. "Well, I'm glad my forgetfulness played a part. I meant to put those back in the matchstick cup, but there was a knock..."

She stopped, suddenly stricken by the memory of seeing Guy again and all that had happened in that brief five minutes in the house. Panic and revulsion swarmed her and it was too much, too fast.

"Oh, Jack, I'm going to be sick."

He grabbed her and ran out of the cave into the snow. She was sick over and over just outside the cave on the white powdery hillside. Sick until all she was doing was dry heaving. She was embarrassed and exhausted and all she wanted to do was curl up and cry. Jack held her and kept her hair back, murmuring soothing phrases in her ear while she retched. Shaking and despondent, she let him take care of her, let him wipe her mouth with snow and carry her back into the cave, let him hold her on his lap and rock her back and forth. She noticed the fire had gotten lower, and Jack fed more of their meager wood into the flames. He covered them with the bedrolls and didn't let her go.

"He was one of them, Jack."

His movements stilled. "Who was one? And who is them?" His voice was calm, but there was a steel edge to his words.

"That man was Guy. I think he was...Hoffman's foreman or something similar. I knew him, Jack. And he knew me, inside and out." She was still so devastated by the memories that she shook all over.

He hugged her to him. "No, he never knew you, Becky. Never. He may have been one of those animals, but he's not a man either."

"I couldn't believe it when I saw him. Tyler warned me, told me someone would come looking for him eventually, but I didn't really listen." She had to speak, to purge the filth from her heart. "The burn scars. That was Guy. He liked to use his cigar to...to..."

He covered her mouth with one cold hand, as if he couldn't bear to hear the words. She worried that she, and not just the words, would disgust him. She pulled his hand away.

"Jack, seeing him again just reminds me of who I am and who I can never be."

We can never be together as man and wife.

"I am so broken inside, I'll never be whole again."

I love you, Jack, but please let me go.

He didn't speak. He simply held her and rocked her as the snow and the wind howled outside. The sound of his heart beating and the warmth of his body lulled her exhausted, pain-wracked body until she slept.

* * * *

Jack had a very tenuous hold on his urge to kill. Only the fact that the woman he loved needed him and was counting on him kept him from tearing back to the Bounty Ranch and killing that bastard with his bare hands.

Jesus, the scars on her breasts were from a cigar. And that...that piece of shit in human skin had done that to her, while he raped her, while she screamed. He felt so impotent, so full of fury, and at the same time, devastated to come face to face with her pain. He wanted to wipe it away, make it so she wouldn't remember, but he knew that was impossible. It was part of who she was, what made her who she was. Perhaps he wasn't man enough to handle a wife with such pain in her past.

Or perhaps his pain was burden enough. He had tried to wipe away that pain, to run from it. It had worked for a long time, but facing it had helped him accept it. Maybe this was Becky's way of facing her pain so she could accept it. No, that wasn't it either. This was her way of making him face her pain so *he* could accept it. Accept what, though?

Jack held her for hours while she slept, alternately shivering and crying. He was afraid to put her down because she was so damn cold. He was afraid for her and so he didn't let her go.

In his heart, he knew he'd never let her go.

CHAPTER FOURTEEN

Tyler, Hermano, and the rest of the Malloy posse arrived at the Bounty Ranch by nightfall. Traveling with them was like being with five Nickys. They all had brownish hair with red mixed in, blue or green eyes, strong noses and chins, and each had the stubbornness of a pack of mules. The snow had all but forced them to slow to a canter, but they kept on until the ranch came into view. Thankfully, the snow stopped just as they arrived. Tyler read the signs of what had happened that day. The barn door was open in the back and hoof prints of at least four horses marked the ground. It was hard to tell because the snow had filled in many of them. There was someone in the house—lanterns were lit and smoke was coming from the chimney.

He dismounted from his borrowed horse and signaled for the others to remain behind the barn. Drawing one of his pistols, he crept into the dark barn and heard nothing. Not a whinny, a nicker, or a human sound. It was empty. He searched the loft and the stalls. Where the hell were Sable and Ophelia? He and Nicky had taken the wagon horses over to the Malloy ranch three weeks ago and left their horses here. If Jack had taken Sable, then did Noah ride Ophelia? That mare should have been about ready to foal, she couldn't take a rider. And Rebecca didn't ride astride, so where was she since there were no sidesaddles on the ranch? Or did those three outlaws kill all three of them and take the horses?

What happened to them?

The barest scrape of a boot sounded behind him and he whirled only to point his gun at Hermano's heart. Hands resting on his own pistols, the bandito looked at him with one eyebrow raised, black eyes glittering in the twilight.

"I told you to wait outside."

"I'm no good at listening, gringo."

Tyler grunted at the understatement then walked back out to the others.

"They're not here and the horses aren't here. But someone is in the house. We're going to split up and approach from all four sides."

Ray seemed ready to do murder. "Any sign of struggle in there?"

"Not that I can see. There's a bunch of shitty tack in one of the stalls though. Stinks like a Mexican whorehouse," Tyler replied. "Snow covered up a lot of the tracks out here, human or animal, so it's hard to tell what happened for sure."

Using hand signals, they all went off to their assigned spots in the house. Everyone was to wait until they heard Tyler and Hermano before coming in, too. Ray and Ethan went to the back of the house, Trevor and John to the north side, Brett to the south side, and Tyler ended up with Hermano approaching the front.

"How the hell did I end up with you?" he hissed.

Hermano shrugged. "*Buena suerte.* How you say, good luck?"

"More like hell's own luck," Tyler growled.

He would never tell the bandito this, but Hermano was as fast as greased lightning and of all of the men in their group, Tyler was glad to have the bandito at his side. Hermano might be a son of a bitch, but he was mean as hell in a fight.

As they approached the house, the darkness hid their movements, and fortunately they were both in black. When they got to the front porch, they each stood to one side of the door and waited. And listened. They couldn't hear any noise coming from inside.

The silence was deafening. Tyler was sure Jack, Rebecca, and Noah had been murdered and left to rot. It would devastate Nicky to lose all three of them. His jaw clenched tight enough to snap a tree.

He held up one finger to Hermano, then two, then three. They both burst through the door, guns raised. Tyler stood high, while Hermano crouched low. Scanning the entry, they saw nothing but some boots and jackets. After a moment, Tyler signaled to Hermano to go to the kitchen while he went in the living room. Holding up one finger to mean one minute, they separated.

* * * *

Hermano found Gaetano on the kitchen floor. His pants were unbuttoned, a knife lay on the floor next to him, and he was quite dead. A blow to the head was the culprit. The blood from the head wound had seeped out to form a dark red, sticky puddle. He'd been dead more than twelve hours by the look of it. He was glad the *bandejo* was dead. Anyone who could hurt a little *chica* like Rebecca deserved what he got.

Hermano took a moment to spit on the body, then searched the pantry and behind the other curtain. He was surprised to find a room in there. The window was open and there were puddles on the floor, like snow had melted and was left there. From someone's shoes, most likely.

Making his way back to the kitchen, he didn't spare the dead outlaw a glance, but went back to the entryway to meet Tyler.

* * * *

There was no one in the living room. And nothing was out of place. Yet something was very, very wrong. He looked up to see Hermano in the doorway.

Walking over, he inclined his head to hear what the other man had to say.

"Gaetano is dead in the kitchen. Looks like someone interrupted his fun with the butt of a gun. No one else is in there, but it looks like someone crawled through the window of the room behind the curtain."

Tyler stared at Hermano. It wasn't what he said. It was that there was absolutely no trace of his "bandito" accent. In fact, it sounded like a Texas twang.

"Where in God's name are you from, *Hermano?*"

Hermano blinked and slipped back into whatever role he was playing.

"From hell, gringo." He smiled and pointed upstairs.

Grimly, Tyler nodded, but promised himself he'd get to the bottom of Hermano's disappearing accent. Together they climbed the stairs, neither one of them making a sound. Strange to find out how alike they actually were. Tyler pushed his way past that thought. Nicky would do a jig if he ever admitted it.

When they got to the top of the stairs, they heard snoring. It was coming from his bedroom. Positioned again on either side of the door, they burst in to find two men sleeping. One was on the bed, the other on the floor. The smell of whiskey and some serious body odor stank up the room. Neither one of them moved.

Tyler used his boot to roll the man off the bed while Hermano emptied the pitcher of cold water on the other.

"Get up, you son of a bitch!" Tyler shouted.

When the outlaw hit the floor, he sat up like a small child and rubbed his head where it had hit the floor.

"What's going on?" he mumbled.

Tyler stuck the gun nearly up his right nostril. "What the hell are you doing in my house, sleeping in my bed, you pile of cow shit?"

Eyes finally wide open, he looked at Tyler with crazed eyes and started babbling. "Mister, I ain't got no idear what I'm doing here. I followed Guy here and now he's dead. Someone done took our horses and it was snowing. So me and Alex here drank the whiskey that was left."

Tyler glanced at Hermano. "I think I should knock him out again."

Hermano had his boot against the other man's throat and was smiling down at him with those empty eyes Tyler remembered too well. He took out his knife with a hiss from the scabbard and waved it in front of the man's terrified eyes.

"You know me?"

The young Mexican man blinked. He couldn't nod or speak because of Hermano's boot.

Hermano's smile grew wider and he lifted up the boot an inch. "*Excelente. Como se llama?*"

"Alejandro."

Hermano's boot landed hard on the man's throat and he started applying more pressure. "Alejandro, eh?"

Tyler didn't want the fleabag to die before he could tell them where the others were. "Might want to ease up a bit on that throat. We need them to be able to actually talk."

Hermano's eyes met Tyler's. He was shocked to see hatred and fury blazing from those black orbs. Like snapping his fingers, Hermano seemed to get ahold of himself instantly.

"*Si*, gringo, we need him to talk."

Hermano stepped away from the man and took a deep breath. Tyler thought he saw Hermano's hands shaking, but it was so brief, he could have imagined it.

Drawing both pistols and aiming them at the men's heads, he widened his stance. "Okay, boys, where are they?"

Neither one answered. The idiot from the bed looked like he was pissing his pants, and the other one was rubbing his throat and staring at Hermano as if he'd seen the devil.

"Let me make this clear," Tyler said, cocking both guns. "I will kill you, don't doubt it. I was a bounty hunter for twelve years, boys. I'm *good* at killing people. I won't even mention how good at it Hermano is. Now, you will tell me where the man, woman, and boy are that were in this house before your filthy, sorry asses got here."

"We didn't see no boy. There was just a woman, a little blonde thing. Guy took her in the kitchen and we heard her screaming. When she stopped, we came downstairs and Guy was dead. We went outside and saw her and a man riding off with our horses."

He swallowed audibly.

"And?"

"And...and so we shot at them, but we didn't hurt no one, mister. They rode off with our horses. Stoled them."

Tyler smiled. "So, when you broke in my house and tried to rape a woman, a friend of mine, that was okay, but two people stealing your probably stolen horses, is not?"

The fool didn't have an answer for that.

* * * *

After they got rid of the body and tied up the other two outlaws in the barn, they searched the rest of the house. Tyler was concerned to find evidence of bandages, lots of bandages. Someone had been hurt and someone else had done some doctoring. There were two cougar pelts in the barn, curing. Which made his worry that much worse. Who had been hurt?

His sheets had been sacrificed to make bandages, so the only bedding in his room was the quilt that now stank like those two idiots. Tyler and the Malloys all put their bedrolls in the living room.

There was hardly any food left in the house either, except for some bread dough that was as hard as a rock. They made do with what they had for the night. Tyler was trying to put together the pieces using the information they'd gathered, but none of it made sense. It sounded as if Jack and Rebecca took off for town, but he was sure they hadn't counted on the snow. He was hoping they'd made it, but it wasn't much more than wishful thinking. He was also worried about Noah. Neither one of the fools ever saw the boy, and he obviously wasn't there, so where was he? And was he okay?

Too many damn questions with no answers. Morning could not come soon enough.

* * * *

Jack had fallen asleep. He hadn't meant to, but he did. He was so exhausted from everything and he wasn't completely healed from his wounds. When he woke, it was to a shivering woman in his arms and a fire that had gone out. It was full dark in the cave. The horses shifted softly, whickering to each other. The wind was no longer howling, which meant it had probably stopped snowing. But it was cold, very, very cold in that cave. All they had were two bedrolls and body heat.

Becky shifted against him. "Jack?"

"I'm here."

"We're going to die, aren't we?"

Why lie now? "I don't know, darlin'. The fire's out, we don't have any food, no matches, but we've got each other."

She spread her hands across his chest, leaned in and began to kiss his neck. "I need you," she breathed against him. "Please, Jack, don't let my last memory be of that monster touching me. Please."

Yes.

Laying her down on one bedroll, he draped the other across his back. She unbuttoned her dress and he unbuttoned his shirt. As her dress slipped off her shoulders, moving gently over her wound, his pants slid down. In moments, they were deliciously nude in each other's arms. She was shivering so badly, he nearly stopped, but when she reached out to caress him, all thoughts of stopping flew out of his head.

She stroked him lightly at first, then with a firmer hand, cupping him, loving him.

"Oh, God, Becky."

She kissed his chest and took little bites at his nipples. He almost came in her hand. Instead, he held her wrists gently, mindful of her injuries, and began to kiss her. Long, slow kisses that made her moan. Tongues danced and dueled over and over while his chest rubbed her nipples and his cock rubbed her mons.

"More."

He licked his way over her cheek and nibbled her ear lobe, sucking it into his mouth while breathing lightly into the delicate shell.

"Jack, that makes me want to come."

Well, he'd certainly taught her the right words.

Licking his way down her neck, he finally arrived at her straining nipples. They were as hard as pebbles. He wished he could see them, see their peach shade so puckered and proud. Instead, he feasted on them like a starving man at a banquet.

Yes.

Her legs spread of their own volition so he rested right in the moist, hot center of her. He had to restrain himself from plunging into that heat. This might be the last time they made love and he wanted it to last.

"Now, Jack, now."

Who was he to refuse her? Sliding in was like coming home. Nothing, *nothing*, had ever been so right for him. She was his home.

He stopped for a moment and laid his forehead against hers. A tear slid down his nose to land on her cheek.

"I love you," he whispered against her lips.

"I love you too." Her voice broke.

He had to start moving or risk losing his fight against his body's urgings.

He tried to go slowly, but his passion overtook them both. The slower he tried to go, the more she urged him on. The heat between them wasn't just from friction, it was the inferno inside him that raged with love and lust.

"Harder, Jack. Harder."

Jack could hold back no longer. He felt for the rock behind her, grabbed on and went for a ride. Rebecca held onto Jack as he plunged over and over; then, too quickly he found his release. It had been fast and wild, exactly what they needed. He tried to move off her, but she held onto him tightly.

"No, don't leave me yet. I like the feel of you inside me."

She moved her hips up and down and he began to swell inside her. His hardness rubbing against her wet softness. "Again?"

Yes.

They made love again, this time more slowly. They kissed and licked and caressed like two blind people trying to memorize each other. It was so sweet, she wept silently and told him over and over again that she loved him. He licked the tears off her cheeks and loved her all the more. Their lovemaking almost felt like a goodbye.

The cave would likely not protect them from the numbing cold. It had been below zero before dark; now it was well below zero. So they kept each other warm through the long hours of the darkness. Giving pleasure and love to keep the sharp teeth of death from taking one another.

At last they were too exhausted to move anymore. Jack dressed both of them as best he could. Becky was like a rag doll, so limp and cold. His eyes stung with grief so deep he could barely swallow. He didn't want her to die, but he could do nothing more to save her or himself. He hadn't rescued her, he'd killed her. Leaving the cave would be suicide, but they'd likely die here anyway. He gathered her up in his arms and wrapped the bedrolls around them as tight as he could.

"I love you," he whispered.

He barely heard her reply. "I love you, too."

He closed his eyes.

CHAPTER FIFTEEN

Tyler heard scraping at the front door. He was up in a flash, gun drawn, crouching in the darkness by the doorway. The firelight didn't reach the corner so he knew whoever was at the door couldn't see him. The door swung open, but all he could see was a silhouette of a man.

The man came in with a grunt and a sigh. He wasn't worried about sneaking in, anyway. He dropped what sounded like saddlebags and closed the door.

Tyler stood to confront the intruder and cocked his gun.

"Mister, you better have a damn good reason for being in my house in the middle of the night. You've got about five seconds before I blow your head off."

"Pa?"

Noah's voice rang in his ears like angels singing. Tyler dropped his gun with a thump and in a second had his arms wrapped around him. He was embarrassed to be so happy to see Noah safe, and at the same time, his heart sang with joy that Noah had called him Pa.

"Noah, son, I can't believe it. You're safe. Where have you been?"

The Malloys were up in a split second, exclaiming over Noah. Tyler brought the boy into the living room to get warm. Hermano leaned down and picked up Tyler's gun. Holding it out to him, the bandito quirked one eyebrow and smiled.

"I think this is yours, gringo."

Tyler snatched it and stuffed it back in its holster. He had never, *never*, dropped his gun before now. But then he'd never had a family before now. Things change.

"What are you doing out in this cold, boy?" questioned John.

"I'm sorry, Mr. Malloy—"

John waved his hand in the air. "Dang it, boy, I told you to call me Grandpa." He resembled Ray in build and coloring, and his blue eyes, surrounded by the wrinkles given to him by countless days on the range, shone with razor-sharp intelligence.

"I mean, Grandpa, when I left town, it wasn't snowing. It blew in fast, and since I was halfway here, I just kept going. I'm wearing long johns and a sweater and my coat. I was cold, but it wasn't too bad. I was even wearing the scarf Mrs. Mal—I mean Grandma—made me for Christmas."

Noah seemed to be okay, if tired and cold. Brett and Trevor went to make some coffee. Everyone was up anyway.

"What were you doing in town all alone? What's been going on here, Noah?"

And so he told them. Tyler listened with incredulity at all that had gone on in the three weeks he'd been gone.

"So, let me get this straight. There was a blizzard that dumped nearly five feet of snow. Rebecca nearly lost her feet to frostbite, but Jack saved them. Ophelia lost the foal. Rebecca was attacked by a female cougar. Jack was mauled by a male cougar. Rebecca killed the male cougar, and then saved Jack's life by doctoring him. You ran out of food and sheets, so you went to town and got caught in snow coming and going. Is that all of it?"

Noah nodded.

"After you left, three outlaws came gunning for me and Nic—I mean your ma. They tried to attack Rebecca, but apparently Jack stopped them and took off with all the horses," Tyler told him.

It all sounded so ridiculous, like a dime-store novel.

"We don't know where they are now, but Rebecca's coat and the boots it looked like she was wearing are still here, along with all the scarves, mittens, and gloves."

Noah's eyes widened. "Do you think they're okay?"

"I don't know, son. Did you see anything on your way from town?"

"I was keeping my head down most of the time, but I thought I might have seen a light near the hills, by the caves, but it was so dark, I couldn't be sure."

The caves. Yes! He'd told Jack about them a while back. If they holed up there, they might be all right. However, the thought of what Rebecca was wearing, or not wearing, in such bitter cold was frightening.

* * * *

They set out at first light. John stayed with Noah, but Hermano and the rest of Nicky's brothers rode out with Tyler. After all, it was their little brother who was missing. The tension in the air was so thick, he could almost see it along with their breath.

The air was so cold it made every part of Tyler want to shrink up and hide. Everything seemed as if it was made of ice. His heart was full of dread of what they'd find at those caves. His head told him Jack was smart enough to keep them alive.

It took an hour and a half to get to the hills. They rode as fast as they dared in the snow in such extreme cold. He'd strapped food, water, extra blankets, and Rebecca's warm clothes to his saddle. It might have been wishful thinking, but Tyler was nothing if not always prepared.

"Where are the caves, Tyler?" asked Ray as they approached the foothills.

"Around the east side, out of the wind at least," he replied, pointing to the right.

"Is there one that's bigger than the others they'd hole up in?" Trevor gazed at the landscape, searching.

Tyler considered for a moment. "There're a couple big ones, but only one tall enough to hold a horse."

He led the way to the bottom of the slope, then dismounted and grabbed the bundle from his saddle. Climbing the incline, he could hear the other five men behind him. No one was going to wait for any news.

He hadn't been a praying man before, but he prayed now. There was no light coming from the cave as they approached. He saw a clear letter J scratched in the stone. That was a good sign. Then he heard the whicker of a horse.

"Did you hear that?" asked Tyler as he turned to look behind them. They all nodded.

"Stop wasting time, Calhoun, move your ass," growled Ray.

Tyler took no offense. Of all the Malloy brothers, Ray was the most like him in temperament. He'd be cursing and yelling too.

At the mouth of the cave, he saw the horses. Ophelia and Sable had been a shield from the wind. He took their reins and led them from the cave, handing them off to Trevor and Brett. The horses seemed to be fine.

Heart pounding, Tyler entered the cave and saw a bundle of blankets set back a bit on the floor of the cave. The remains of a fire were in front of the bundle, but it obviously had gone out a while ago. That was bad. Really bad. He heard Ray's indrawn breath behind him and knew he'd seen the cold fire. A man without a fire on a bitter night like last night was asking to die.

Tyler approached and knelt next to the bundle. He could see Jack's boots poking out from beneath, and the hint of a woman's shoe behind. Swallowing a lump in his throat, he reached out and pulled the blanket back.

Jack and Rebecca had their arms wrapped around each other. They were both so pale and lifeless. Their clothes were wrinkled and some appeared to be on backwards. He didn't want to speculate, but it looked like they'd been keeping themselves warm the old-fashioned way, using body heat.

"Are they alive?"

He wasn't sure which brother had asked the question, but it was time to find out. He pushed Jack's shoulder.

"Jack, wake up."

No response. He jiggled the shoulder a bit harder. "Jack, wake up."

Still no response. From behind him, someone's breath hitched.

Ray shoved past him and slapped Jack on the cheek. "Get up, Jack!" he yelled.

Jack's eyelids fluttered open and his fist came up flying to clip Ray on the jaw. Ray fell back on his ass. "What the hell?" Jack mumbled.

Tyler grabbed hold of Jack's arm. "Jack, it's Tyler. Wake up."

Jack blinked slowly like a man waking from hibernation. "Tyler?" He tried to focus his gaze on him, but he looked confused and disoriented.

"Becky?" Jack whispered. He leaned down and cradled her in his arms. "Becky, darlin', wake up."

Becky darlin'?

He shook her and lightly patted her cheek. "Come on, darlin'. My family came to save us. Wake up now."

He shook her a bit harder. Tyler was astonished to see tears rolling down Jack's face.

"We only had two matches and the fire went out. There wasn't any food or water. I—I did the best I could. We tried... I can't... Becky, *please.*" He was crying in earnest now. He hugged her close to his chest and started rocking.

Tyler felt the prick of tears behind his own eyes. God couldn't take such an angel when she was so obviously loved.

"Jack?"

He ignored Tyler and continued to rock Rebecca. Ray got up and crouched down next to him, touching his shoulder.

"Jack, let me take a look at her."

Jack shook his head violently. "No, I killed her just as sure as I put a gun to her head. Nobody touches her but me."

"Dammit, Jack, let me look at her. There might be something we can do."

Jack lifted his head and looked at his brother with agonized eyes. "She's so small, Ray. So cold."

Ray began to pry Jack's arms from around her. "It's okay. It's okay. Let me see her."

Jack reluctantly loosened his grip. Ray placed his hands on her neck and then held her wrist. He smiled at Jack. "She's alive, brother. Barely, but she's alive."

The joy on Jack's face was nearly enough to make all of them cry. Hermano shoved his way through with firewood. He quickly laid out a fire and started it. Tyler was glad someone was there who didn't get caught up in emotions. A fire was exactly what Jack and Rebecca needed.

Tyler unwrapped his bundle of blankets and clothes and they began to work on Rebecca. The army of Malloys was unleashed. Hot coffee, firewood, and lots of helping hands. There was a tear in Rebecca's sleeve and if he wasn't mistaken, dried blood, too. And her hand was bandaged up. They all took turns warming her feet and hands, careful not to make her injuries any worse than they were. Jack would not let her go completely so they had to work around him. Trying not to burn her, Tyler dribbled hot coffee into her mouth. She swallowed, which was a very good sign.

After fifteen minutes, she began to get some color in her face. Jack was fighting off his well-meaning brothers as they tried to get hot coffee down his gullet. All he wanted to do was hold Rebecca.

"We need to get her back to the house, Jack."

Ray held Jack's arms while Tyler gently picked up the slight woman. Jack fought and growled at his brother.

"Get a hold of yourself, Malloy. You're too weak to carry her. Get your ass on Sable and let's get back to the ranch."

Jack slumped on the floor, all the fight out of him. He looked up at Tyler then focused his gaze on blanket-wrapped Rebecca.

"She can't die, Tyler. If I let her go, she might die." His voice was barely more than a whisper, and thin with his pain.

"I won't let her. I promise you that."

Jack seemed to accept Tyler's promise, albeit reluctantly. He let Ray help him stand and put on warm outer gear, then they all headed for the horses. Hermano extinguished the fire and followed them.

* * * *

The ride back to the Bounty Ranch took almost two hours. Tyler didn't want to strain Jack too much and each man took a turn holding Rebecca in front of him. He didn't want to wear out any of the horses or the Malloys. Hermano even took a turn, although he seemed to have lost his sardonic edge over the course of the day. He was looking mighty serious and a lot less cocky. Tyler sure did wonder about that.

When they arrived, Tyler was not surprised to find Nicky there. Less than a month until she was due to give birth and the woman was a force of nature. He wanted to yell at her, but instead he just smiled into her worried eyes.

"They're all right, magpie, just very cold."

"I wired the sheriff. He should be here anytime."

"That's good. Can you brew up some hot coffee for them?"

She nodded and waddled back into the house. Noah stood on the porch, wide-eyed and silent. Tyler asked him to take the horses to the barn and get them rubbed down, warning him to steer clear of the outlaws in the far stall. Noah had the reins in his hands before Tyler even finished speaking.

Family. This was a family. People helping each other, loving each other, and being there whenever, wherever they were needed. He glanced at Hermano to find his gaze very pensive. He'd definitely have a talk with the bandito later.

Ray was holding Rebecca. Tyler dismounted and held up his arms to take her, but Jack was there, pushing him out of the way.

"I will carry her in," he growled, wobbling a bit on his feet.

Tyler frowned, but nodded at Ray. He took up position behind Jack to catch them if they fell. But Jack didn't lose his grip on the small woman. He clutched her and headed inside.

"Jack?" he heard her whisper.

"Yes, it's me, Becky."

"Where are we?" Her voice was slurred.

"Bounty Ranch. My family came and found us. We're okay, honey, we're okay."

She reached up to touch his cheek. He closed his eyes and almost stumbled. Tyler reached out to stop him, but Jack righted himself immediately. The love shining in Rebecca's eyes more than answered Tyler's questions. Somehow the two of them, who were at odds as long as they'd known each other, had fallen in love. Nicky would be beside herself.

"Don't let me go, Jack."

"Never."

* * * *

Tyler had threatened to sit on Jack to make him stay on the sofa in front of the fire. He wanted, no, he absolutely *needed*, to go see Becky upstairs, but Tyler reassured him that she was just fine, to let Nicky take care of her.

Jack felt like crap physically. His hands and feet hurt, as did his ears. He was weak, and still a bit woozy. As he sipped hot coffee with whiskey, he glared at his brothers. Ray, Ethan, and Trevor were assigned to watch him. Like a naughty kid who had been caught snatching cookies from the jar. He resented it and he let them know it in no uncertain terms.

"Just shut up and drink, Jack," growled Ray. "Babysitting you isn't high on my list either. I'd rather be shoveling horse shit in the dead heat of summer."

He scowled at him. "Nice. Makes me feel very loved, big brother."

Ethan, ever the practical peacemaker, had to speak up. "Jack, we just want to make sure you're okay before you get any sicker than you are. For God's sake, you said yourself it's been less than three weeks since the cougar tried to take you apart."

Jack grunted and continued to drink the coffee. He had to see her, had to touch her. He was lost, running through a maze, and only she could help him find the way out. They didn't understand. None of them. He had almost gotten her killed. Oh, God, that was so painful to admit. He almost killed her. The woman he loved above everything, and his stupidity had nearly taken her life.

Tyler came into the room, bringing a blast of cold air with him from outside.

"Horses seem to be fine. Thanks for keeping them in the cave with you, Jack. They wouldn't have survived outside," he said as he took off his coat and gloves.

Jack harrumphed. "They wouldn't have been in any danger if I wasn't stupid enough to set off in a snowstorm."

Tyler sent a glance to the brothers, who quickly left the room with excuses about things to do. He sat on the sofa next to Jack who was looking down at his hands clasped between his knees.

"Jack, when Hermano came to your pa's ranch to let us know about Guy, I have to tell you, I was worried. That was one bad-ass outlaw, out to kill me and Nicky. You're a rancher, not a gunfighter, and the odds were not in your favor. We nearly rode the horses into the ground to get here."

"You don't have to remind me that I'm not as good as you, Tyler. I know I'm an idiot and a coward," Jack interrupted, his resentment building.

"That's not what I'm trying to say, dammit. I'm not very good at this," Tyler rubbed his hand down his face. "I wanted to say that you kept Rebecca alive, you saved her. You didn't know the storm was coming, you didn't know we were coming. You acted on your instincts and saved her life. And in the process, killed one of the men who had hurt her so badly. You're no coward and you're not an idiot. You saved her."

Jack didn't agree, but he was wasting his breath if he tried to argue with Tyler. There was only one person in the world more stubborn than Nicky and that was her husband. If that's what he thought, there was no changing his mind. But Jack knew better. He'd be lucky if Rebecca was even speaking to him after nearly dying in his care.

His breath got trapped in his chest at the thought of losing her because of this. He prayed she would forgive him.

"Whatever you think. Do you think I can lose the babysitters now?"

Tyler nodded and left the room.

Jack couldn't sit there any longer. He threw off the blankets, gulped down the rest of the coffee and rose. He had to grab the sofa for a moment to stop the room from spinning. Setting the mug on the floor, he decided to sneak upstairs to see her. He had to. Without Becky's touch, he couldn't live.

* * * *

Rebecca was warm. Blessedly, incredibly warm. Bundled up in bed with hot water bottles, blankets, wool socks and hot tea. Her hand and arm were freshly bandaged and only throbbed slightly. She felt so lucky to be alive, and now was reveling in being warm again. It was nearly nightfall and she hadn't seen Jack since they'd arrived. Tyler had pushed him out of the room. She wondered where he was.

She heard about the outlaws, and felt nothing but relief to know Guy was dead. She felt no joy in his death. The sheriff had finally arrived and taken custody of the other two.

Nicky bustled in, very, very pregnant, with another plate of food. Rebecca smiled at her friend.

"Where's Jack?"

Nicky's eyebrows shot up. "Downstairs, getting warmed up by the fire."

Rebecca was embarrassed to feel herself blushing. "Is he okay?"

Nicky nodded.

"Well, good." A moment of awkward silence had her scrambling for something to say. "You look like you're about to drop that baby any minute."

Nicky grimaced. "Sure feels that way, but I think it's going to be a bit longer. I'm glad to be back home, though. I wanted to have our baby here."

After setting the plate on the dresser, Nicky helped Rebecca sit up. She was still sore and felt weak.

"Do you want me to feed you?" Nicky asked.

Rebecca shook her head. "No, I think I can do it myself now. My hand feels much better."

Handing her the plate, Nicky lowered herself onto the chair and got comfortable. Rebecca gazed at the delicious-looking fried chicken, potatoes, and biscuit. She dug in with relish, though mindful of her sore hand.

"So, were you able to find out from Jack what was bothering him?" Nicky rubbed her belly.

Rebecca nearly choked on the biscuit.

* * * *

Jack made his way up the stairs as quietly as possible. Luckily no one saw him. He hoped his damn brothers were far enough away to not stop him from reaching his goal. Rebecca. He was nearly there, almost at her side. When he heard Nicky's question, he paused outside the half-open door.

What the hell was she talking about?

Rebecca didn't answer immediately. It sounded like she was choking on something. After a few moments, she cleared her throat and spoke. "Jack and I became friends."

Nicky huffed in impatience. "That's good, but he still looks like hell. Oh, I know, I know, don't curse. But truly, I didn't know if it was from being out in the freezing cold all night, or if he was still having nightmares."

Nicky had told her about his nightmares, dammit. That was his business, not hers. Jack knew he shouldn't be eavesdropping on their conversation, but he couldn't stop. It was as if he *had* to hear what Becky was going to say. He had a feeling it wasn't going to be good.

"I don't think he's having nightmares anymore."

"And did he talk to you?"

"Yes, he did."

"Christ, Rebecca, this is like pulling teeth. Did you get it out of him?"

Jack held onto the wall for support. This could not be real.

"We talked, and...and he did share with me what was bothering him."

"And?"

"He told me in confidence, Nicky. I don't think it's my place to tell you."

Nicky snorted. "You wouldn't have even gone near him unless I asked you to. Even then I had to convince you to do it. Jack doesn't even like you."

He closed his eyes against a wave of pain. Sweet Jesus. Nicky forced Rebecca to get close to him? Did she pretend all this because of Nicky? Was that all it was? A favor for a friend?

"It's true he didn't seem to like me. He went to a lot of trouble to avoid me, but—"

"But nothing. You two were alone here for almost three weeks. You had to have pried something out of him."

"Yes, you did ask me to find out what was bothering him. And I did. That's the end of it. There isn't any more. It's done."

He couldn't listen anymore. The pain in his heart was nearly suffocating him. He stumbled back down the stairs and out into the night, without a coat or a hat. Blind, deaf, and dumb to everything but the agony tearing through him like the cougar's teeth.

That's the end of it. There isn't any more. It's done.

* * * *

"Oh, please. Tell me what he said."

Rebecca frowned at Nicky. "No, I will not. Jack is not only my friend, but we became very close while you were gone. In fact...I love him, Nicky, and I won't betray him for anything."

Nicky's mouth opened in a silent O of astonishment at Rebecca's proclamation.

"You *love* him?"

Rebecca smiled and nodded. "Yes, I do. And I think he loves me, too."

Nicky laughed and clapped her hands. "I can't believe it. I'm so happy for you."

She leaned over and hugged her. Rebecca's sadness had sunk its teeth in deeply, overshadowing her happiness. She knew she could never be married to Jack. He'd never want a wife like her, someone broken and used up. Her time with him had passed. But oh, it was the best time of her life. The sweet memories were enough to last her a lifetime.

"Are you going to be my sister now?"

Rebecca shook her head. "I can't marry him, Nicky."

She looked affronted. "What are you talking about? If you both love each other, why not?"

"I can't saddle him with a wife who's as scarred as me. I can't just wash away all these," she said, holding up her wrists. "Or my memories. I...I just can't."

Nicky waved her hand in dismissal. "I don't believe that's true. Love is the most important thing. Everything else is secondary."

Rebecca wished she could believe that. "It's not enough."

Nicky frowned at her. "I never thought you were a coward, Rebecca."

With that pronouncement, she left the room. Rebecca stared after her in astonishment. Was she taking the easy way out because the hard way would mean giving up the heavy load she'd been carrying for more than four years? Was she truly being a coward?

* * * *

Jack ran out to the barn. Tyler was there, currying Sable. He stopped and glared at Jack.

"Seems like you're dumb enough to risk dying again when you come outside without a coat, Jack. Nicky's going to whoop your ass, not to mention what your big brothers will do." He started towards him.

Jack held up his hands in a warning gesture.

"Fuck you, Tyler. Leave me the hell alone," he snarled hoarsely, climbing the stairs to the loft.

If Tyler had any reply, Jack wasn't going to listen. He crawled into his bed and pulled the blankets over his head. He needed to be alone. To lick his wounds. To come to terms with the fact the woman he loved had been getting close to him at the request of his sister. His *sister*, for Chrissakes.

How could he have been so stupid?

When had a woman ever really wanted him for himself? Not once before Becky. Before *Rebecca*. Most women got close to him to get closer to one of his brothers. Jack was secondary; he had never been first. Until now. And that wasn't even real. They'd been pretending, playing house like kids.

And then he almost got her killed. She would never consider marrying him after that, even if he loved her enough for both of them.

Stupid, stupid, stupid.

He'd left his heart open for the excruciating agony crushing him now. He didn't know a person could feel such pain without actually dying.

* * * *

Tyler went into the barn and lit a fire in the potbellied stove for Jack. If the danged fool wanted to be out here alone, the least Tyler could do was make sure he didn't freeze to death. He stared at the unmoving lump under the bed, heard what he thought was a sob, then shook his head and left.

Walking back to the house, he wondered what had driven Jack out to the barn. He'd been so intent on getting to see Rebecca. When Tyler went inside, he found Nicky just entering the kitchen with a disgruntled look on her face. She waddled to his side and pressed herself, as close as she could, to him and inhaled deeply.

"Mmmm, I love the way you smell."

"Okay, if that's what you like, I'll try to smell all the time."

She giggled into his chest. "You're silly, bounty hunter."

He kissed her temple. "Jack ran out to the barn a few minutes ago, without a coat."

She reared her head back and looked at him. "Why?"

He shrugged. "Dunno. I lit a fire for him. But he's huddled under his blankets like a mole so I left him there. Figured he needed some time to himself. Too many people around here."

He knew he sounded grumpy, but Nicky just smiled and cupped his cheek with her warm hand. "You *would* think my brothers were 'too many people'." She chuckled. "Should I go out and talk to Jack?"

He frowned. "Nah, I'd let him alone until tomorrow."

"Okay, but first thing, I'm going out there and finding out more of what happened between him and Rebecca."

"Magpie..."

"Nope, don't even 'magpie' me—I'm going to get those two together if it's the last thing I do."

Tyler shook his head. When a woman was happy with her man, she thought everyone deserved to be happy. He wasn't going to stand in the way of a hotheaded redhead who was eight-months pregnant and faster than lightning with a gun. No sirree. She could talk to Jack until the cows came home.

Whether or not Jack would be talking back, or even listening, Tyler had his doubts.

CHAPTER SIXTEEN

Jack was gone when Nicky arrived at the barn to talk to him the next morning. He had left a note on his bunk that said "Gone Home". Nicky went into the kitchen to tell the rest of her brothers. Ray looked murderous when he found out and threatened to string Jack up by some body part for going out in the cold after almost dying less than two days before. Called him a name she didn't want to repeat, even in her own head.

"That little bugger. I'm going after him," Ray announced to the family sitting around the kitchen table. He stood, pushing his chair aside as he started toward the door. "Ethan, Trevor, Brett, you coming?"

Looking longingly at Nicky's biscuits, they all hurriedly shoved food and coffee into their mouths. They gathered up their gear and followed Ray out the door. Nicky packed up the rest of the biscuits with some ham and bacon. She wrapped a bit for each brother to carry on the ride home, then kissed them all and sent them on their way.

"You'll let us know when the time comes, right?" Ray asked, the last to leave.

She patted his shoulder. "We'll send Noah."

Ray nodded then abruptly enfolded her into a fierce hug that brought tears to her eyes.

"Thank you for coming when Melody was born. I don't think I ever said that. Things are so mixed up, Nicky. I...I'm sorry."

She hugged him back. "No thanks and no apologies needed, big brother. I love you. Where else would I be when you need me?"

Ray's green eyes looked suspiciously moist when he pulled away, then shook Tyler's hand.

"Take good care of my baby sister, Calhoun."

Tyler raised an eyebrow. "Someday you might trust me."

Ray snorted. "Someday I might."

With that they were gone as quickly as they'd come, in a thundering pack of horses. Nicky closed the door and hugged Tyler quickly. "Let me go tell Rebecca."

What she really wanted to do was kick Jack's ass.

* * * *

Rebecca smiled when Nicky came in. The wary, sad look in her friend's eyes melted the smile off her face.

"What's the matter, Nicky? I just heard a bunch of horses. Did your brothers leave?"

Rebecca picked at the quilt, afraid to hear what Nicky was going to say. She sat down heavily on the side of the bed and wrapped Rebecca in a hug. Rebecca hugged her back, desperate for the love, terrified for the reason it was being given.

"Jack's gone," Nicky said quietly.

Rebecca's heart stopped beating. She couldn't have heard Nicky correctly.

"What do you mean? Did he ride back with your other brothers?" Rebecca hated that her voice shook.

Nicky pulled back and looked into her eyes. "I'm not going to lie to you or try to give you some lame excuses. He ran, plain and simple. He was gone before the sun came up. Hell, he may have left in the middle of the night for all we know. He left a note."

Rebecca's heart leapt at the mention of a note.

"It just said 'gone home' and nothing else."

Oh, it was worse than she thought. Her heart didn't just stop beating; it burst into a million jagged pieces, tearing her up inside. It hurt so damn much.

"Why?" she whispered.

"I don't know, sweetie. I don't know."

Nicky held her while she cried her eyes out. Jack had left. Without a word, and riding along with him was her wounded heart and soul. She would never be the same.

After Nicky went back downstairs, Rebecca lay in the bed feeling sorry for herself, holding her little wooden angel like a talisman. In truth, she felt numb, detached from everything. Nicky brought meals up and reminded her to eat. She didn't even bother to dress or brush her hair. She just sat in bed, the bed in which she and Jack had first made love, held her wooden angel, and stared out the window nursing her pain, recovering from almost dying. And nearly dying inside.

His leaving spoke volumes about how he truly felt about her. After reuniting with his family, he must have realized how much trouble she was, how hard it would be to have a woman with such a past. The horror of coming face to face with a part of her pain, the sobering reality that he had killed a man because of her.

But even through the pain caused by his running away, she remembered the joy of being held in his arms, of sharing her heart with him. And it was a tiny bit to nourish her battered soul, to bring herself back from despair. He had given her a gift. And now it was time to stand on her own two feet and live the rest of her life. Alone.

After she accepted that fate, life was livable again. The next morning, she rose from the bed and picked out clean clothes to wear. It was time to stop grieving and move on.

* * * *

A week passed. Rebecca busied herself completing all the sewing she had intended on doing, including some new sheets for Nicky. She never discussed why the sheets had been torn up. Doing so would open up the wound she had carefully stitched shut on her heart. Hermano stayed on the ranch, keeping an eye on her, which made her feel oddly safe. He doted on Nicky and made sure if Tyler wasn't around he was. Hermano told Rebecca over breakfast one day he was making sure baby Calhoun arrived safely. Oddly restless, the bandito kept himself busy helping Tyler finish the addition to the house.

She laughed and talked with her friends. Behind it all, she nursed her wounds, inside and out. Her palm healed neatly, as did the bullet graze on her arm.

Rebecca had just finished stitching a gown for the baby. It was a pretty white sleeping gown with just a hint of lace around the collar, made of flannel for the cold winter evenings. Sitting on the living-room sofa, she folded the gown, feeling full of self-pity for the babies she would never make sleeping gowns for, flannel or cotton. She could kick herself for being so pitiful.

Nicky waddled in, holding her back, an obvious wet stain on the front of her dress.

"Talk to me, Rebecca. I think it's time."

Rebecca jumped up and guided Nicky to the sofa. She laid her hands on Nicky's protruding belly and felt the extreme tightening of the muscles.

"Oh, crap, that hurts." Nicky groaned and punched the sofa hard.

"You are surely in labor, Mrs. Calhoun. Do you want me to go find Tyler? I think he's working on that part of the corral fence that came down in the storm."

Nicky shook her head. "No, he'd just be in the way and hovering over me. Let's get ready to bring this baby into the world, first."

Rebecca agreed with Nicky. "You're right. First things first, let's go upstairs."

They walked upstairs with Rebecca guiding her friend slowly as they made their way to Nicky's bedroom. There she helped the expectant mother into a clean nightdress.

"You might feel better if you walk around a bit," she told Nicky. "I'm going downstairs to get the supplies we'll need."

Nicky nodded and started pacing, muttering under her breath about Tyler's punishment. Smiling, Rebecca went downstairs to the kitchen. She was reaching for the sharp knife when the memory of the last time she held it nearly slapped her in the face. She roughly pushed it away. Today was about life, and death had no place here.

She gathered the clean bandages she'd used with Jack, the blanket Mrs. Malloy had crocheted for Nicky, a change of clothes for the baby from the pile of freshly laundered ones, and the knife. Upstairs, Nicky was still pacing. Rebecca deposited everything on the dresser and went back for water.

She was just headed upstairs with the pitcher of hot water from the reservoir on the stove when the front door swung open and Tyler walked in. He glanced at her, then at the pitcher of hot water and frowned. He slammed the door behind him and bracketed his hips with his fists.

"What's going on?"

She clung to her devotion to her friend instead of her friend's husband.

"You're not needed yet, Tyler. We've only just begun. It will be hours before you should to be there to hold her hand."

All the blood seemed to leave Tyler's face. He even swayed a bit on his big feet as his hands dropped to his sides.

"Nicky's...having the baby? Now? It's early yet. Doesn't she have a few more weeks?" he croaked.

She set the pitcher on a step carefully, then walked back down to him. Stretching up to reach, she placed her hands on either side of his face and forced him to look her in the eyes. She didn't need two patients.

"I can't take care of your wife and child and worry about you toppling over like a fallen oak. You're too doggone big to move. If you feel faint, sit down and put your head between your knees. If you feel like you need to do something, boil some water." She removed her hands and stepped back.

He rubbed his hands over his face; then closed his eyes. "I'm scared, Rebecca. What if something happens to her? I can't... I wouldn't... Jesus."

She patted his shoulder. "Don't worry. Everything will be fine. Nicky's strong and healthy; nothing will happen to her. No doubt your baby will be as healthy as can be."

She turned to go back upstairs.

"You'll call me...when she needs me?" He swallowed audibly. Rebecca was surprised to hear a tremor in Tyler's voice.

"Of course. She will need your support, if not your hands to smash."

"My *hands*?" she heard him repeat as she scurried upstairs.

* * * *

"I want to talk to you about something," Nicky began.

Rebecca was busy washing her hands and the knife in hot water. "What do you want to talk about?"

"You seem to avoid touching my belly, yet here you are, ready to help me give birth to my baby. Are you...that is...are you still thinking about...your baby?"

Rebecca's blood ran cold. Nicky must have known Rebecca had been pregnant, but Nicky never asked what happened to the child, and Rebecca had never mentioned it. Friends knew when not to ask a question.

"Talk to me."

Sighing, she set everything on the dresser, dried her hands, and then went to look out the window at the beautiful snowy landscape. "You never asked me before."

"Now seemed like a good time. I need to take my mind off the pain, and it seems like you need to tell me something."

Ever since she'd told Jack the whole truth, it had gnawed at her conscience that Nicky didn't know. There wasn't much she didn't share with her. Somehow Nicky had known she needed to talk about her own baby.

"I gave her up for adoption."

Nicky came up behind her and put a hand on her shoulder. They were both silent for a moment.

"It was a girl?"

Rebecca nodded.

"That was a very brave thing you did."

She turned to look at her friend as if she'd lost her mind. "Brave? I could not have been a bigger coward."

Nicky shook her head. "No, you're no coward."

But Rebecca felt like a coward. She had never even breathed a hint of her darkest secret to Nicky until now. Until Nicky had forced the issue. Yellow bellied, that's what she was.

"Do you know what happened to her?"

"No."

"Do you ever wonder?

Every day.

"I try not to think about it, Nicky. No matter if you think I'm brave or not, it was a time in my life that I'd just as soon put behind me where it belongs. Can you understand that?"

Nicky looked a little taken aback.

"I'm sorry. I don't know why I just snapped at you. How about you sit on the edge of the bed and I'll rub your back?" Rebecca felt badly for how she'd spoken to Nicky, but she couldn't seem to stop herself. Just to speak of her daughter brought excruciating pain, something she'd had enough of.

Nicky frowned, then sat on the bed with a grunt and a curse aimed at her husband.

* * * *

As it happened, Tyler didn't need Rebecca to call him when it was time. Nicky's screeching his name brought him on the run. He must have taken the steps three at a time. It had been a long night. The pink of the sunrise was just beginning to paint the sky when Nicky began to push.

Rebecca helped all she could and Tyler encouraged Nicky and held her hands, only grimacing when she really squeezed.

Just as the sun shone in the window, baby boy Calhoun slipped into Rebecca's waiting hands. He was beautiful, pink, and perfect, and bellowing to bring the house down. He had dark hair like his daddy.

"You have a son."

Tyler's hungry gaze drank in the little boy, flailing tiny arms and legs and shouting.

"He's beautiful," Tyler breathed, his voice hoarse with wonder.

"More, Rebecca, there's more. I'm still pushing. Help me."

Rebecca quickly cleared the baby's mouth and nose, and then cut the cord. She swaddled the baby deftly and handed him to Tyler.

"Clean him up, but keep him warm."

She had a feeling there was about to be another Calhoun born. Ten minutes later, baby girl Calhoun arrived with as much pomp and circumstance as her brother. She was healthy, just as loud, with dark hair like her brother. Not quite a matched set, but close enough.

"It's a girl."

Tyler looked like she'd hit him with a tree limb.

"Another baby?"

Rebecca barely held the urge to roll her eyes and smack him. "Tyler, twins obviously run in the Malloy family. Your wife is a twin."

He shook his head and cradled his son as Rebecca cleaned up his daughter. She finished and laid the warm bundle next to her exhausted mother.

"Your daughter, madam."

Nicky was crying as she held her daughter for the first time. Tyler laid the baby boy on her other side. They looked at the babies and then at each other. The love flowing between them could have moved mountains. It was so poignant, tears pricked Rebecca's eyes. It's what she wanted with Jack, but it was not to be.

She quietly cleaned up Nicky, then took all the dirty linens and left the family alone. Her part was done. Life had reaffirmed itself.

* * * *

They named the boy Logan Francis, and the girl, Rebecca Belinda. Rebecca tried to demur, but Nicky stood firm. Her daughter would be named after the two best girlfriends in the world. The babies were healthy, thriving children, doted on by their parents and their big brother. Nicky and Tyler asked Noah if they could adopt him. Never had Rebecca seen such happiness in one house. The Calhouns were incredibly lucky to have each other.

Two days after the birth of the Calhoun twins, Hermano left without a word. Apparently before Tyler could speak with him, judging by his loud cursing and complaining. The bandito had written a note for Nicky that she didn't share with Rebecca, but Rebecca understood he had needed to leave for his own reasons. At least he had written more than two words. He had also left a small silver rattle and two gold pieces for the babies. A gift Tyler could not begrudge his children, even if he did grouse about it. Tyler disappeared for about four days after that, and came back grunting at Nicky that he'd found "him" and delivered her message.

In a few weeks, Nicky was back to normal, taking care of the babies. She used a dresser drawer for baby Rebecca until Jack could build another cradle.

Jack, the talented woodworker, the love of her life, the hole in her heart. Rebecca tried not to think about it, but it was so hard. Every time she rocked Logan in his cradle, she imagined Jack's hands gently tapping in the inlays and smoothing the wood. Every time she rubbed the little wooden angel in her pocket, she was reminded of the man who had made it for her.

It was time to go back to Nebraska. Time to go home.

Tyler and Nicky argued with her, asked her to stay. Rebecca knew she had to go. She was a fifth wheel; the Calhouns were complete without her. In the midst of the new family, she felt out of place and very lonely. Real life called her. Life without Jack.

* * * *

She was packing her things when Nicky came in and sat on the bed. Now that she wasn't pregnant anymore, she happily donned her jeans every day.

"Are you sure I can't convince you to stay?" She raised her eyebrows with a hopeful expression.

Rebecca shook her head and smiled. "No, I've been away from home too long. And you don't need me anymore."

Nicky took her hand. "I'll always need you, Rebecca. You're my friend and I love you."

Hugging her quickly before she burst into tears, Rebecca forced herself to remain bright.

"I'll be ready in just a few minutes. Is Tyler getting the wagon ready?"

"Yes, he's just about done." Nicky paused, tracing the pattern on the quilt with her finger, not meeting her eyes. "Rebecca, before you go...I need to talk to you about Jack."

Rebecca tensed and felt the familiar weight of disappointment settle on her heart. "I can't."

"Yes, you can," Nicky insisted. "If you could bottle and sell the sadness I see in your eyes every day, you'd strike it rich. I'm your friend, Rebecca, and he's my brother. It's too hard to be in the middle, in the dark, and not know what happened. You told me you loved each other and then he left without a word. It was so odd and so unlike him. I can't help but wonder...what happened?"

Rebecca sat down heavily and stared at the dress in her hands. It was the one with the pink rosebuds, Jack's favorite. Without warning, a tide of sadness welled up and spilled over, right out of her eyes in a torrent of tears. Nicky held her as she struggled with her emotions. It was so hard, so hard to be strong and to accept what she couldn't change.

Tyler poked his head in and looked horrified to find Rebecca crying. Nicky waved her hand at him and he disappeared in a blink.

"I'm sorry, Nicky. It's difficult to talk about it."

Nicky waited patiently for Rebecca to continue, stroking her back and holding her hand.

"I didn't mean to fall in love with him," she said as she wiped her eyes with a clean handkerchief from her bag. "I always thought he was handsome, but somehow being together for weeks, we learned about each other and found something missing. Life. That was what was missing. *Living.* Being with Jack made me a whole person, and I feel as if half of me is missing again with him gone. We healed each other. I know I'm not a catch with my past, my scars, my obvious lack of fortune and beauty, but I thought Jack saw past all that. I think when that man...Guy came, it reminded Jack of how painful my past was. It forced him to confront life with a woman like me. It would be too hard for him."

"Too bad Jack's not here to tell us why he left. I sure would like to know."

Rebecca silently agreed.

"Did you...well, were you really together? Tyler said in the cave that you looked...well like you'd been *together.*"

"Oh yes, we were. It was what I needed to get over my fear of men, to learn passion and love. Our time together was beautiful."

"Does he know about...you know, about the baby?"

She sucked in a quick breath. "Yes, I told him everything."

"And he ran."

"Apparently."

"I'm going to be blunt, Rebecca, because I can't be anything else." She paused. "Could you be pregnant?"

Rebecca's eyes widened at the possibility. It had been a while since she'd had her courses. If she were, it would be the most precious gift she'd ever received. A child made from love.

"No," she lied.

Nicky considered her face for a moment with narrowed eyes, and then nodded. "Are you angry with him?"

Rebecca shook her head. "I'm not angry. I'm just...I miss him. I love him. He will always own my heart."

"I'm glad you're not angry. Because I'm angry enough to kick his ass from here to California and back."

Rebecca looked at her friend in shock.

"And you can bet when I get my hands on him, he'll know it."

* * * *

Rebecca tried to reason with Nicky, but she wouldn't listen. She almost felt sorry for Jack—almost. But he had run without even saying goodbye.

She was getting ready to leave. Noah carried her bag down the stairs and stopped to wait for her. He looked incredibly nervous and was practically bouncing on the balls of his feet. What was this about?

"Miss Becky, I mean Miss Rebecca... I ah...wanted to talk to you before you left," he said, his voice cracking up and down. She felt sorry for the boy.

"Yes, Noah, what is it?"

He finally raised his eyes to her and she saw what he was going to say before he spit it out. Oh, Lord. She had to stop him.

"Well, I wanted to say that I—"

"I'm going to miss you, too, Noah. You are such a sweet boy, on your way to being a man. The girls will be flittering around here like bumblebees on a handsome flower. I'll bet your new mother will have to beat them off with a stick," she burbled as she slipped her gloves on. "You were a wonderful friend and helper, Noah. We wouldn't have survived, any of us, without you."

She hugged the shaking boy, who blushed the color of a radish. Walking briskly out the door, she heard Noah sigh long and loud before he followed her out.

Fortunately, she had headed off the declaration of love she was sure the boy would have blurted out. Her own heartbreak was enough to handle.

Noah loaded her things into the wagon. Nicky was holding Logan and Tyler was holding baby Rebecca. She kissed and hugged the babies, then kissed Tyler's cheek quickly. She would swear he even blushed a bit, but he leaned down and let her do it. Nicky handed Logan to Tyler and clasped Rebecca in a fierce hug.

"Oh, I'm going to miss you so much, Rebecca," she said. "Even if my lunkhead brother never marries you, you will always be my sister."

Rebecca choked back the tears that threatened. "I'll miss you too. Take good care of your family, Nicky. They are more precious than any prize."

She climbed into the wagon with Noah's assistance. Tyler returned the babies to Nicky and climbed up next to her. She turned and waved as they pulled out of the yard. Life was going to be back to normal again.

But normal meant no love, no passion, and no Jack.

CHAPTER SEVENTEEN

Jack was scared. Scared absolutely shitless. He drove the wagon with his mother—still gorgeous at her age—the spitting image of Nicky, only more mature. They were on their way to the Bounty Ranch to see Nicky and the babies. It was all his mother had talked about for weeks. Another cradle was strapped in the back for his new niece, Rebecca. Each time he heard his mother say the name, his heart clenched and he had trouble breathing. The rest of his brothers suddenly couldn't help bring the cradle to the baby. So, he had to do it. Miserable, scared, and falling apart with each slap of the horses' hooves. Each mile brought him closer to Becky, back to the betrayal.

He didn't want to see her. He didn't know what he'd do if she was still there. Part of him wanted to get down on his knees and beg her to marry him. The other part was still raw and wounded after learning she had gotten close to him at the request of his sister. He should have said goodbye, but he couldn't. So he had run, like the coward he was. He had run from everything difficult in his life, and Becky was no exception. Only it was more than difficult. It had almost killed him.

The last month had been a blur. He'd worked himself nearly to death not only making the cradle, but also fixing everything wooden that even had a bent nail. His father kept looking at him like he wanted to ask him what the hell he was doing. His brothers steered clear of him, after Ray had given him one clip to the jaw. Said it was to teach him a lesson in his own stupidity. He hadn't said anything about Becky, and Jack hadn't asked. He wondered if she was okay, if she was happy with him gone. He tortured himself daily imagining what she was doing at that moment.

And the nights...oh the nights were the worst. He no longer had nightmares. Instead, he had erotic, pulse-pounding dreams that woke him up so hard, he could have hammered nails with his cock.

But worst of all...he missed her. He missed talking with her, playing chess with her, just being with her, touching her. It was hell.

God, he didn't want to be back here. Where she was. But here he was. His heart was pumping so hard, he thought it would crack a rib or two.

His mother was practically dancing on the seat. His father rode alongside the wagon with a smile on his face, watching his wife.

"You'd think you'd never seen a baby before, Francesca. Ray's little Melody is only a few months old. You get to see her all the time."

"It's not the same thing, John. These are Nicky's babies. My baby's babies."

His father shook his head and just continued to smile.

Jack hadn't smiled since he left Becky. He doubted he could. At that moment, he wondered if he could even breathe.

When they arrived at the house, Jack was so tense he had to restrain himself from shoving his mother and the cradle out of the wagon and running back the way he came. Or simply jumping from the wagon and running. Anything but facing Becky again.

But she didn't come out of the house. Only Tyler and Noah came out to greet them. He sat on the wagon bench, gripping the reins, unable, unwilling to get down.

After shaking his father's hand and kissing his mother's cheek, Tyler had Noah bring them in the house. He turned his gaze on Jack and looked once again like the fierce bounty hunter who had chased Nicky down. Cold, hard, and mean.

"She's not here. She went back to Nebraska two days ago."

The breath whooshed out of him. He couldn't say if he felt more relieved or sad.

"But I'm warning you now, the only reason I'm not pounding you into the ground is that your sister wants the privilege."

With that, he turned and went into the house.

Jack turned the wagon toward the barn, to take care of the wagon and the horses. All the while trying to convince himself that he wasn't hiding from his sister.

* * * *

Within twenty minutes she found him. He was just finishing putting away the harnesses from the horses in the tack room and taking his sweet time doing it. Cursing under his breath, he pretended not to notice her, tapping her foot, sure she was giving him the dirtiest look she could muster.

"Jack, don't ignore me."

He glanced back at her, trying to look uninterested. "Oh, hey, Nicky. Congratulations on the twins. Hear they're sweeter than honey."

She looked as if she was going to punch him. "Never mind the babies. You have a lot to answer for, Jackaroo."

He decided to opt for the angry tactic. "It's none of your goddamn business, Sissie. So stay out of it."

She leaned in close, sparks flying from her green eyes. "Yes, it is my business. She is my best friend and you are my favorite brother."

She poked him in the chest with each word. And those fingers were sharp. He grabbed her hand to stop the poking.

"But it doesn't involve you."

"Yes it does!" she shouted; then looked as if she might cry. "Jack, you broke her heart."

Embarrassingly, his throat began to close up and tears pricked his eyes. "No, you've got that backwards. She broke mine."

He walked out of the tack room, intent on leaving the barn as quickly as possible. Unfortunately, he wasn't quick enough. She clutched his arm in a surprisingly punishing grip.

"Oh, no, you don't."

He tried to pull away. "Let go, Nicky."

"Not a chance. Now you listen to me." She turned him around and forced him to look her in the eye. "You ran. You ran like a yellow-bellied coward, Jack. I have to know why. She told me everything."

He snorted. "Yeah, I'll just bet she did."

She narrowed her gaze. "What does that mean?"

"I heard you. I heard you talking about how you asked Rebecca to find out my 'secrets', and that she only came near me because you asked her to." He was shouting now. "What did you say? Something like 'You wouldn't even go near him if he was the last man on earth.'"

"That's foolish talk, Jack. I never said such a thing."

He was so angry, so full of hurt, he didn't watch his tongue. It all came pouring out. "You asked her to spy on me. How could you, Sissie? You...you made me fall in love with her, to tell her everything, to make love for the first time in my life. To a woman I thought loved me. I laid my heart and soul on the table like a lovesick calf. And it got thrown in my face. I can't believe you did that, Nicky."

He wrenched his arm out of her grasp and stomped off blindly. Not caring where he was going, just away from her, away from the reminder of his pain.

"Jack, wait."

He didn't slow down. If anything, he walked faster, and soon he was running through the snow, stumbling blindly, falling and getting up. But running. He barely noticed there were tears on his cheeks.

Suddenly Ophelia was in front of him, blocking his path. He reared back and fell flat on his ass. Nicky jumped off the horse—of course, she was riding bareback—and dropped down beside him. She grabbed him in a hug and wouldn't let go until he stopped struggling. Sighing, he waited until she let go, then he was going to get up and run again.

"Jack," Nicky said, looking at him with teary eyes. "I don't know what to say. What you heard...that wasn't what happened. It's true I asked her to find out what was bothering you, but that was it. I didn't ask her to find out your...secrets."

He didn't believe her for a minute. She must have seen it in his eyes.

"I was desperate, and I was worried. I didn't know any of this would happen. Jack, you must have heard us talking. Didn't you hear her tell me how much she loved you?"

Well, no, he hadn't heard *that* part.

"She told me to mind my own business, that she wouldn't tell me a damned thing about you or your secrets. And then she told me she loved you. She loved you enough to tell you her secrets. You know about the baby. You know about her fears and her pain. How could you think for even a minute that she was pretending?"

Jack stared at his sister in shock and began to realize that he was quite possibly the dumbest person in Wyoming.

"She said she loved me?"

Nicky closed her eyes and nodded. "Yes, she did. She told me she loved you and missed you. This is all my fault, Jack. I started this, and the two of you, the most important people in my life besides Tyler and the babies, were caught in the middle of my own stupidity and got hurt. I'm so sorry, Jack."

"She said she loved me?" he repeated, feeling more and more like the village idiot.

Nicky opened her eyes and smiled. "Oh, yes, she told me she loved you on the day she left. That was two days ago, Jack. She also told me she isn't angry. She thought you ran because you couldn't be with a wife who had such a hard past, a wife who had given away her baby for adoption. She seemed to accept a life without you, like it was the easy way out."

"She loves me."

Nicky smacked him on the arm. "Would you stop sounding like such a fool? You have to get her back. There aren't two people more perfect for each other in all the world."

He felt like he'd just been kicked by a horse. But his heart was a hundred pounds lighter. And best of all, he was starting to feel the one thing that he needed. Hope.

"Do you think I can get her back? Do you think she'll marry a half-time rancher, half-time furniture maker?"

She smiled. "You could be a full-time furniture maker with your talent."

"Help me, Nicky. What should I do? I can't go tearing off after her. I don't think she'll listen to me."

"You'll need to find a way to mend that heart of hers, Jack. And I think I know what to do."

CHAPTER EIGHTEEN

Rebecca counted the days again. There was no mistake. She had not had her courses in two months. Dear Lord, she was going to have a baby.

She dropped like a stone into the kitchen chair, clutching the calendar in her hands. Staring at it, but not really seeing it, there was nothing but joy in her heart over the realization. When Nicky had asked her nearly four weeks ago, she pushed the thought aside, not because she was afraid, but because she didn't want to contemplate such a thing, then have it snatched out of her hands.

Her time with Jack had been precious, a gift she would treasure always. Each night, she had incredibly sensual dreams that featured Jack. Sometimes she imagined things they had never done. She woke up hot, her nipples straining against her nightdress and her mons throbbing with heat. Once, she touched herself to see if she could ease the ache. It had helped a bit, but it wasn't the same.

Rebecca missed Jack. She missed him so much it was almost too much to bear. In fact, at times she would turn to talk to him, to tell him something, but he wasn't there. Belinda was looking at her like she needed to reevaluate her cousin's sanity. More than once, she assured her that she was just fine. Just fine.

But not really. Life was like a shadow of itself without him.

Her little wooden angel he had carved for her never left her pocket. It was her talisman, her armor against the crushing melancholy pervading her days. She hadn't expected it to be so hard without him. But it was. So hard.

* * * *

The next morning, she was looking at the patterns for baby clothes when there was a knock at the front door. Belinda seemed to have disappeared, so Rebecca set the patterns aside. A second knock sounded before she could get there. Slightly annoyed at whoever was so impatient, she flung open the door.

And nearly fell on her fanny. The last person Rebecca thought she'd see on her doorstep was Jack Malloy. He had broken her heart so thoroughly nearly two months ago, seeing him now ripped open a wound that had begun healing. The pain and the joy swirled together in her heart. She held onto the door so she wouldn't throw her arms around his neck and beg him to be hers. The other hand was tucked deep in her pocket, rubbing her wooden angel.

Jack's eyes seemed to drink her in like a man dying of thirst. He didn't smile, or even blink. He just stared.

"Hello, Jack," she said.

He started at her voice. "I'm sorry, Becky, I don't mean to stare at you so. You...you just look so damn, I mean darn beautiful. I feel like it's the first time I'm seeing you all over again. It just snatches the voice right out of me."

His voice was low-pitched and so full of wonder she felt herself leaning toward him. Snapping her spine straight, she managed to keep her gaze steady.

"Why are you here?"

He stared down at his feet as they shuffled around a bit.

"I came for two reasons. The first is to apologize to you from the bottom of my toes to the top of my head for being such a jackass. I have a hard time trusting people and when I should have believed in you, trusted in you, I broke faith with you. I can't tell you how sorry I am. I misunderstood something, but Nicky set me straight, and I...I don't have an excuse for running like a coward, without a word to you. Please forgive me, Becky."

She opened her mouth to accept his apology but found her voice had been snatched away as well. Instead, she nodded.

He breathed a huge sigh of relief and wiped his forehead with his hand, which was shaking.

"And the second reason?" she croaked out.

Dropping down on one knee, he took off his brown Stetson and held it to his chest. His eyes gazed up at her solemnly.

Oh, dear God.

He took a deep breath and shifted his knee on the porch. "The second reason is to ask you...is to ask you if you would..."

He cleared his throat. "That is...will you, only if you want to, of course...um...marry me?"

The earth paused for a moment as Rebecca looked down into Jack's blue, blue eyes. Eyes that held her future, her love, her very soul. How could she possibly ever say no?

"Because you see, I love you, Becky. I love you so much it hurts to think of us ever being apart. And I need you, more than I need my next breath. In fact, I don't even want to breathe if I can't be with you. I've only been half-alive for the past two months. You are my life."

She dropped down on her knees and wrapped her arms around him.

"Yes, yes, a thousand times yes. Oh, Jack, I love you, too."

He picked her up and twirled her around the porch until she was dizzy, all the while shouting "Yahoo!" over and over.

"Oooh, Jack, stop, I'm going to be sick." She laughed.

He hugged her tightly one more time, then set her back on her feet. "You won't ever be sorry."

She smiled. "Never. Not once."

He took her hand and led her to the edge of the porch. "There's one more thing."

Looking toward the road, she saw a carriage sitting in front of the house. It was a nondescript black carriage with a gray horse pulling it. Inside she could see a woman.

"Who is that?" she asked.

"You'll see," he answered without really answering.

Curiosity was about to bite her on the tail by the time they got close to the carriage. She saw the woman was not alone. There was a small child in there, too. A little girl, judging from the look of the bonnet. Her heart began to pound in giant thumps that rattled her feet.

"Who is that?" she repeated, a strange, dizzying sensation starting to unfurl in her chest.

This time Jack didn't answer her. When they reached the carriage, he made her stand by the fence. Reaching in, he helped the woman down, then picked up the little girl and set her next to the woman. She was a little thing, probably only two or three, dressed in a black wool coat and green bonnet. Shiny black shoes and white socks completed the outfit. The woman was probably about Rebecca's age, with brown hair and warm brown eyes, wearing a gray wool traveling suit.

"Becky, this is Mrs. Morton. Mrs. Morton, this is Rebecca Connor, my fiancée," he said, introducing them.

Rebecca held out her hand to Mrs. Morton and they shook briefly.

"I'm happy to meet you, Miss Connor. Mr. Malloy told me you intend to marry this weekend."

Rebecca glanced at Jack with a raised eyebrow and he had the decency to look somewhat chagrined. Glancing back at Mrs. Morton, she said, "Yes, we do."

"Wonderful. All we need to do now is sign the papers and I can be on my way."

Rebecca turned toward Jack, the need for an explanation climbing up her throat. He knelt down by the girl and held out his hand. A little pink hand was placed trustingly in his. He straightened and walked the three steps over to where Rebecca stood. Her heart had climbed to her throat and tears were pricking behind her eyes.

Who was it?

"Becky, I'd like you to meet Hope. Hope, this is Miss Connor."

Her knees failed her. She dropped down next to the child and came face to face with her own gray eyes staring back at her from underneath the green bonnet. A sweet, cherubic face and angel-kissed lips curved in a smile.

"Please to meetchoo," she said shyly.

Rebecca couldn't speak. She couldn't utter a sound. This was her baby, her child, her miracle who she had thrown away three years ago. And Jack had found her.

"We can sign the adoption papers inside, Mrs. Morton," she heard Jack say.

Adoption. She had never dared voice her dream before. Her deepest wish for her daughter to be hers again. Yet here she was...within reach, near the heart that had never stopped loving her child. Jack gently pulled on her elbow to help her stand, and then held out his arms to Hope. She willingly went into his arms and perched on his hip. Together they looked at Rebecca expectantly.

"How?" she managed to whisper.

"Help from Belinda, from Nicky, from my father. And a whole lot of door pounding." He shrugged. "In the end it was luck. Hope's adoptive parents passed away about a month ago from influenza. I was lucky I found her when I did. There were two other couples interested in her. I explained to Mrs. Morton that she was your cousin's child and she agreed that a blood relative would be ideal for adoption."

"I saw the resemblance right away, Miss Connor. I'm glad Mr. Malloy came to see me," said Mrs. Morton.

The broken pieces of her heart, long ago shattered by life's cruelties, fit together again in that brief, shining moment. He had truly made her whole again. This was life. This was love.

"Ready?" He smiled and held out his hand.

She nodded and took his hand. "Yes, I am."

Together they walked back to the house. Belinda was standing in the doorway, smiling and crying at the same time. Rebecca smiled back at her, not believing how wonderful this moment really was.

When they reached the porch, Jack set Hope down. She reached up her little hand and took Rebecca's.

"Hope, do you like angels?"

"Yes, ma'am. My mama and papa are angels. I like them just fine."

She smiled down at the child of her heart, then up at the love of her life.

"How do you feel about a little brother, Hope?" she asked with a smile.

She heard Jack curse as he walked into the doorjamb behind them.

"Dammit, what little brother?" Jack shouted.

Rebecca smiled and walked forward into life. Into living again.

BETH WILLIAMSON

You can't say cowboys without thinking of Beth Williamson. She likes 'em hard, tall and packing. Read her work and discover for yourself how hot and dangerous a cowboy can be.

Beth lives just outside of Raleigh, North Carolina, with her husband and two sons. Born and raised in New York, she holds a B.F.A. in writing from New York University. She spends her days as a technical writer, and her nights immersed in writing hot romances for her readers.

To learn more about Beth Williamson, please visit www.bethwilliamson.com or send an email to Beth at beth@bethwilliamson.com.

Look for these titles by Beth Williamson

In ebook

Available Now!
The Bounty
The Prize
The Reward

Coming Soon
The Treasure ~ July 2006
The Gift ~ November 2006

In Print

Available Now!
The Bounty
The Prize

Coming Soon
The Reward ~ September 2006
The Treasure ~ October 2006
The Gift ~ February 2007

Has Hermano stolen your heart?
Enjoy this excerpt from

The Reward
(c) 2006 Beth Williamson

The Malloy Family series continues. When the bastard bandito Hermano returns home to confront his past, he finds a future he never dared to hope for. Available June 13, 2006 at Samhain Publishing...

Malcolm was unloading broken and worn fence posts from the back of the wagon behind the barn. He was dirty, sweaty, and the sight of him made her heart skip a beat.

He'd taken his shirt off and that chest was enough to make her knees turn to jam. Tan ribbons of muscle covered with whorls of curly black hair. Drops of sweat traveled down those nooks and crannies, meandering a path she wanted to follow with her hands. Or perhaps her tongue.

A beautiful specimen of a man. Damn, Malcolm sure had filled out since he was eighteen. Leigh had to resist the urge to reach out and touch.

Then he turned to return to the wagon and she saw his back. She must have gasped or croaked or something because he whirled to face her. Gloved hands fisted, sweat streaming down his face, black eyes snapping. When he saw it was Leigh, he relaxed.

"*Amante,* my wolf, you should not sneak up on me like

that."

Her mouth was as dry as the Texas wind. His back. *Oh, Jesus help me.*

"I am not fit for a lady's company yet. After I finish, I need to go down to the creek and wash."

She nodded. "I... I... Okay sure."

His eyebrows drew together. "Are you okay, *amiga*?"

"I, uh, came to tell you... That is, to ask you. See, there's plenty of stew and biscuits..."

He smiled. A brilliant white slash in the dark, beautiful face.

"Ah, *si*, a supper invitation. *Bueno.* I will be there in fifteen minutes."

He turned and grabbed another load of wood from the wagon, presenting her with his back again.

Stomach churning, she turned and fled back to the house. She almost fell into the kitchen, and nearly landed on her head.

Leigh pulled off her glasses and slammed them in her shirt pocket. She furiously pumped the handle in the kitchen sink. She grabbed a wash rag and held it under the stream, soaking it in cool water. Great, gasping breaths were jumping out of her like grasshoppers in a brush fire. Out of control and frantic.

She wrung out the excess water and pressed the wet cloth to her face, then slumped to the floor.

Get a hold of yourself!

It wasn't working. Lord, it was *not* working!

Leigh knew something had happened between Malcolm and

Damasco, and that Malcolm had been punished. It was the reason he left. Now she knew what his punishment had been. And she wished she didn't.

Malcolm's back was covered with scars from a whip. Covered from his shoulders to his waist. Every square inch of his skin had been flayed from his young back. The sheer brutality of how anyone could do that to another human being made her heart hurt. To think that it was done to her dear Malcolm made her heart weep.

She didn't know how long she sat there, with the cloth pressed to her face.

"*Amante.*"

He was there, crouched on the floor next to her, and she hadn't even heard him come in. He pulled the cloth away from her face and cupped her cheek with his hand. His black eyes were full of concern. His wavy hair was sprinkled with drops of water. The tips brushed his shoulders leaving what looked like tears on his clean brown shirt. Lord, she had never stopped loving him.

"What is wrong?"

Leigh had never been one to mince words. "Your back. I'd never seen it before."

His eyes hardened. "It's not pretty, *si*? Ah, well, the señoritas in the cantina don't mind."

Behind his flippant words, she heard ancient pain. Oh, Malcolm.

"I'm not usually such a sissy," she said wearily, clambering to her feet. He rose from a crouch fluidly.

"You are no sissy, *amiga.*"

She shook her head. "Sissy."

He smiled. A real smile that was so blinding, she nearly did weep.

Sissy.

"No sissy. A woman."

With that pronouncement, he cupped her other cheek, then lowered his lips to hers. At the first touch, she nearly jumped out of her skin. After a few gentle, nibbling kisses that made even her feet jitter, he let go and stepped back.

"Let us eat, *amante.*"

A strong woman, fighting against the odds to protect her family...

Kitty McKenzie
(c) 2006 Anne Whitfield

Suddenly left as the head of the family, Kitty McKenzie must find her inner strength to keep her family together against the odds.

Suddenly left as the head of the family, Kitty McKenzie must find her inner strength to keep her family together against the odds. Evicted from their resplendent home in the fashionable part of York after her parents' deaths, Kitty must fight the legacy of bankruptcy and homelessness to secure a home for her and her siblings.

Through sheer willpower and determination she grabs opportunities with both hands from working on a clothes and rag stall in the market to creating a teashop for the wealthy. Her road to happiness is fraught with obstacles of hardship and despair, but she refuses to let her dream of a better life for her family die. She soon learns that love and loyalty brings its own reward.

Enjoy this excerpt from Kitty Mackenzie

Kitty sent Mary up to make dinner for the children as closing time drew near. From the back room she heard Connie and Alice talking as they cleaned. She moved a chair and swept under a table and allowed her mind to dwell on Benjamin.

Why did he have to announce their engagement?

She shook her head at his logic. Did he not realize she would have to face everyone by herself? Stifling a sigh, she turned to sweep under another table when an elegant carriage and pair halted outside the shop window.

Georgina Kingsley paused on the carriage step and stared at the shop frontage. Kitty sensed the other woman's loathing. It emanated from her like an aura. Georgina waited for her groomsman to open the shop's door before regally gliding in. She surveyed her surroundings with cold blue eyes. Her gaze rested on Kitty as though it wished not to. "I'm not here on a social visit."

Determined to be gracious, Kitty summoned a small smile. "I'm sorry to hear that, Mrs Kingsley."

"I'm here because of the announcement published in *The Times* this morning." Her disdain etched itself onto her pale face. "You have seen it, I suppose?"

"Yes."

"My husband and I had not been consulted. Benjamin made no mention of an engagement before he sailed."

"I understand, but before you ask, I didn't place the advertisement."

"My son wouldn't have done it without speaking to me or my husband beforehand." Georgina's upper lip curled in contempt. "So, who does that leave?"

"No one of my acquaintance, Mrs Kingsley. I promise you." Kitty struggled to keep check on her temper. "Benjamin must have done it."

Georgina stared at the ring on Kitty's left hand and her eyes narrowed into slits. "Where did you obtain that?"

"This ring was given to me by your son, Mrs Kingsley. It is my engagement ring." She was so thankful of the empty shop. Her embarrassment would be complete if customers saw this spectacle. She suspected Connie, Mary and Alice waited in the back room ready to come out and help her if need be.

"That was his grandmother's engagement ring!" Georgina's face lost its alabaster hue and grew pink. "She willed it to him to bestow upon the woman he is to marry."

"Then, I'll wear it with pride."

Georgina sucked in a deep breath. "You, Miss, will not wear it at all! You will never marry my son. He deserves better than a penniless snippet like you!"

"That is enough." Kitty put up her hand. "I love your son and he loves me. We *will* be married the minute he returns from Australia and there is nothing you can do about it."

Connie, Mary and Alice marched in to stand at her back, forming a small but angry defense.

Georgina Kingsley tilted her head majestically. Her lips thinned into an angry mark on her face. "I can completely assure you, Miss McKenzie, that in no way will you and my son ever be joined in matrimony. If it takes every day of my life in making sure it does not happen then I'll do it. That is my pledge." She turned on her heel and strode out to her carriage. The driver whipped up the horses and it jerked into motion and out of sight.

"My God," Connie whispered and placed her hands on Kitty's trembling shoulders. "Aw lass, you've got a right dragon in that one, an' no mistake. Come out back an' have a cuppa."

Kitty sat silently while the others fussed and discussed the Kingsley woman. She longed for Benjamin's strong arms to comfort her and his tender words to confirm his love for her, but they were many miles away. She would just have to dream of them. But oh, how she missed him already and it hadn't even been a week. How would she survive eighteen months?